TANGLED LIGHTS

AND

SILENT NIGHTS

Merry Christmas!

BRENDA VICARS — KATE BIRDSALL — KELLY STONE GAMBLE —
MICHAEL MEYERHOFER — CLAUDE BOUCHARD — NICOLE EVELINA —
CIARA BALLINTYNE — GAIL CLEARE — VICTOR CATANO — REECE TAYLOR —
DIANE BYINGTON — KELLEY KAYE — DARREN R. LEO — ERICA LUCKE DEAN
— STACEY ROBERTS — LETEISHA NEWTON — DEBBIE TENBRINK —
CEE STREETLIGHTS — TIMOTHY WOODWARD — JUSTIN BOG

COPYRIGHT AND LICENSE INFORMATION

Each story within this collection is protected by copyright of the author.

Cover designer: LeTeisha Newton, Beyond DEF
Project Coordinators: Kelly Stone Gamble; Tiffany Fox; Beyond DEF
Interior Layout: Deena Rae Schoenfeldt; E-Book Builders

IN THIS VOLUME

When Polarity spends Christmas Eve with Ethan's family, she discovers a side to him that she never knew. In a single moment, the unlikely combination of a deadly rattlesnake, a ten-year-old's tears, and "O Holy Night" awakens Polarity's understanding of Ethan, her own heart, and love.

In this Christmas mystery, we follow Cleveland Detective Liz Boyle out of the squad room and into her personal life, where we see glimpses of her humanity, that she often conceals.

All Cass Adams wants for Christmas is a new pair of boots, but her husband, Roland, has other plans. From the *USA Today* Bestselling novel, *They Call Me Crazy*.

A condemned man learns that not everyone is cut out to be a hero. A tie-in to the award-winning fantasy novel, *Wytchfire*, Book I in the Dragonkin Trilogy.

From *USA Today* Bestselling Author of the Vigilante Series. What better time than Christmas for the Vigilante to show some heart?

Aspiring suffragist Victoria Woodhull has finally secured an entre into New York high society thanks to an invitation to Christmas Eve dinner at Cornelius Vanderbilt's house, but her low-class family threatens to ruin everything. A tie-in to the award-winning novel *Madame Presidentess*.

Another Bloody Festival
by Ciara Ballintyne
Epic Fantasy

Desperate to be the world's leading research wizard, the genius Alloran makes a fateful decision that ends in bloodshed and changes the course of the world's future. A short story prequel to *The Seven Circles of Hell.*

Holiday in Hartland
by Gail Cleare
Women's Fiction

It's Christmas Eve at the lakeside cottage in Vermont where Bridget Reilly has been living alone. Soon her daughter Lizzie, born twenty-five years ago and adopted by the birth father's family, will arrive for their first holiday together in this continuation of Cleare's *USA Today* bestseller, *The Taste of Air.*

Some Carry-Tail: A Gabriel & Orson Story
by Victor Catano
Urban Fantasy

Gabriel's quest to find his witchy girlfriend, Sheila, the perfect Christmas gift gets derailed by a family swindled by a street Santa. It's up to him and Orson, his magical bulldog, to set things right.

A Twin Oaks Christmas
by Reece Taylor
Contemporary Romance

Featuring Hannah and Lee from *Bless Your Heart.* Celebrate the holidays in the town of Twin Oaks at the annual Christmas Festival. It is a fun-filled time with a heart-warming, unexpected family reunion.

A Jewish boy with a girl's name discovers a Christmas miracle. His mother is not happy about it. From the autobiographical *Trailer Trash with a Girl's Name*.

From International Bestselling Author of *Whispers in the Dark*, featuring the beloved Caesar St. Clair of *Vanquished*. Ashlyn gave Caesar everything he ever wanted—love, marriage, a son, and the darkness he craved. Now he's on a mission to give her the world for the holidays.

Featuring Lieutenant Jo Riskin from *Warped Ambition*, a Jo Riskin Mystery. When Jo meets a young runaway on Christmas Eve, she's determined to reunite him with his family and help them give each other the most important Christmas gift of all.

When Natalie takes a job as an elf at Santa's Enchanted Forest, her cynicism toward the holiday becomes overwhelming. Now, after eating one of Santa's Christmas cookies, Natalie must accept that perhaps not everything about the holiday is exactly what she thinks it is.

Sean Jackson is determined to come out to his dad over the holidays. Will the spirit of Christmas help his dad accept Sean's sexuality, or will Sean's coming out ruin the holiday for his whole family? A continuation of the ALA Rainbow List novel *If I Told You So.*

Seeking redemption, a mother of two daughters examines her past, makes a bold change to her present, and hopes for a future not haunted by her memories. "And Mercy Mild" is linked to the story "Hark," from the holiday collection *Hark: A Christmas Collection.*

LIFEAFTER

THE LIFEAFTER PROJECT IS A PATHWAY TO AWARENESS.

Created by world-renowned Rock and Celebrity Photographer, Michael Strider, partnering with Supermodel Julie Anderson and entrepreneur Brian Whitfield. The trio has a goal fueled by a passion, that passion is to shatter the stigma and spread awareness to three taboo topics that underscore society today: Suicide, Substance Abuse, and Domestic Violence.

The term LifeAfter was born from the idea there is life after any problem someone may have, no matter how severe they feel it may be. We believe that no matter the problem, things can and will get better. With your help, together we can ensure that those in need see that light.

Proceeds from the LifeAfter Project will fund organizations that have a positive impact on suicide prevention, drug addiction, and domestic abuse.

OUR MISSION

The LifeAfter Project aims to reach out and provide assistance for those who struggle with thoughts of suicide, substance abuse, or domestic abuse. All these things are related to mental illness. Our goal is to educate, inspire and spread awareness. We hope that our efforts will help eradicate the stigma associated with this insidious epidemic.

http://lifeafterproject.org/

TANGLED LIGHTS
AND
SILENT NIGHTS

The Moment I Knew I Would Love Ethan Forever

BY BRENDA VICARS

We were only sixteen, but in one moment I knew I would love Ethan forever. It happened at his grandmother's farm two days before Christmas. His grandmother had invited us to a cookout—just our family and his. It was at the end of a warm December day. That sounds weird—*warm December*—but in south Texas warm days and nights in the Christmas season are common. We had finished eating and everyone was sitting on the back porch in lawn chairs drinking iced tea and watching the dying embers in the barbeque pit glow orange wavers among the black charcoal and ashes.

Ethan's chair was next to mine, and I was hoping now that the meal was over and the sun was setting, we would take a walk alone, steal a few minutes. My family would be leaving town the next morning, and this was the last time I'd be with Ethan for weeks or even months. He had whispered to me earlier that we'd take a walk after dinner. But neither of us had anticipated how his youngest sister, Keisha, would attach herself to me. To her five-year-old mind, I was a delightful new playmate. Braced with her favorite doll and a handful of tiny dresses and accessories, she wedged herself between my and Ethan's chairs.

She dropped the wardrobe items onto my lap. Her dark brown eyes, so much like Ethan's, darted from the clothes to my face and implored me to love this game as much as she did. She thrust a pink dress at me. "This is Ellen's favorite outfit." She watched as I looked it over.

"Oh!" I turned it from side-to-side. "Beautiful."

Ethan, from behind Keisha's back grinned at me. Unlike most guys his age, he didn't need to roll his eyes or put on a macho show of being disinterested in his sister's childish play. He honored her interests with the same respect he'd give someone his own age.

Keisha stripped her doll and took the pink dress from me. "Now when she puts on her ball gown, we have to take her to the palace to dance."

I helped her slip the doll into the new outfit. "That sounds like fun."

As soon as the doll was dressed, Keisha grabbed my hand and tugged. "Come on. The palace is this way." She angled her head toward a gazebo about twenty feet from the house.

I laughed. "Okay, we're going on a journey to the palace?"

"Yes." She glanced over her shoulder at her ten-year-old sister. "Theresa, you can come, too." Keisha paused to wait until her shy sister pushed herself up from her chair.

I didn't think Theresa had said a word during the whole visit, and every time I tried to bring her into a conversation, she shrank into herself.

Ethan stood as if to come with us, but when we stepped to the edge of the porch, Dad said to him, "How about if I help you lift the grill and clean it? I think the pit has cooled enough."

Keisha, still clasping my left hand, led me off the porch. I stretched my free hand out to Theresa, but she seemed not to see me. She kept up with us, but she walked several feet to my right.

There were dozens of cedar fence posts, at least seven feet long, lying parallel in rows on the ground in front of the gazebo as if someone were planning to build a fence. Stepping carefully onto a post, Keisha dropped my hand so she could stretch both arms out to mimic balancing on a tight rope. She walked across the posts. "This is the moat around the palace. Be careful and don't fall into the water. There's alligators and monsters in there."

I started walking across them as well. Each post moved a little as I stepped on it, but the posts were so close together that their rolling motion was blocked by the next posts. After a couple of steps, it was easy to balance and follow along. "Whoa. Alligators and monsters? Are you sure it's safe?"

Theresa giggled. I had never heard her do that before, and even in the dimming light, I could see that she had a big smile. She said something softly as she held up her arms to do the same exaggerated, balancing walk that Keisha and I were doing.

I couldn't pull my eyes off of Theresa as I continued stepping across the posts—it was so cool to see her finally having fun. "What did you say, Theresa? I couldn't quite hear you."

Her eyes met mine.

My stomach lurched.

The post under my foot mushed and rolled. It gave way as if I had stepped on someone's leg instead of hard wood. A sizzling buzz hissed from my left. It was the tail of a rattlesnake, vibrating. To my right, between Theresa and me, the snake's fist-sized head lifted. I had stepped on the middle of a long rattlesnake stretched out between two posts. The snake, at least five feet long, gaped its mouth wide open. Its fangs were too close to Theresa. She stumbled backwards onto her back on the ground. Her head raised. She stared at the snake's darting tongue inches from her feet.

I'm not sure how, but suddenly I was holding a squealing Keisha, high off the ground with my left arm, and I was reaching toward Theresa with my right. She watched frozen, staring at the snake organizing its body into a coil.

Ethan materialized, with his back to me, between the snake and me, holding a long stainless-steel barbeque fork in one hand. I was relieved that he was with us but terrified he would get bitten. He bent over the snake. His broad back and shoulders obscured my view of his hands, but I could see the tines of the fork in front of the snake's head. Ethan was luring the snake or distracting it with the fork. I sensed, rather than saw, Ethan's hands moving, slowly and then with shocking fierce force. In a flash the snake's head whipped out and away from Theresa, the long fork dropped to the ground, and Ethan took several side steps. In the dim light, he held the snake's struggling tail with both hands, just high enough so that the head was still on the ground.

The snake scrambled to crawl away, but all it could achieve was a desperate, continuous zig-zag motion on the ground with its head. Ethan moved farther away from us, one sure step at a time, never taking his eyes off the snake, never giving the snake more than its small piece of earth to work against. When he reached a sidewalk bordered by a low stone wall, Ethan stopped walking. Slowly, he took one hand off the snake. He waited a few seconds as if to make sure he could manage to keep his hold with one hand. With his free hand he reached down to the wall, grasped a large rock and brought it down with frightening force onto the snake's head. He struck the head two more times making it a flattened smear on the cement.

Dad stepped up with a shovel and pressed it onto the snake's body just below the head. "You can drop it if you want. I'll hold it until it stops."

Ethan dropped the snake's tail, and the body whipped around, seeming as strong as it had been when it was alive. Ethan's mother took Keisha, now chattering about the snake, from my arms. Mom wrapped her arms around me.

Ethan squeezed my shoulder with one hand. "Are you okay?" His voice was clear and steady.

"Yeah." My voice shook.

He looked over my shoulder toward his mother. "Where's Theresa?"

"She's okay," his mother said. "I checked her. Thank God, no one was bitten." She stepped forward, still holding Keisha, and reached for Ethan.

He accepted her embrace. "Where is she? Theresa?"

His mother looked around for her and said, "Maybe she went into her room."

Ethan pulled away, "I'll go see her."

Ethan's grandmother stepped a little closer to Dad, who still had the writhing snake clamped down with the shovel. "I'll put some kindling on the barbeque coals—make a little fire to burn the head so none of the pets get ahold of the fangs or poison glands."

Ethan pushed back out of the house, letting the screen door slam behind him. "She's not in there."

Everyone stilled, even Keisha stopped her retelling of the snake story.

For frantic minutes we darted in all directions, calling Theresa's name and searching the grounds with flashlights and cell phones.

I collided with Ethan's mother in front of the house. She glanced at me with a start and punched at her phone. "I'm calling 911."

Ethan's voice came out of the darkness. "I've got her. She's okay." He walked past us carrying Theresa like a baby. "She was in her climbing tree." We followed him around the side of the house to the back porch. He settled into a chair with Theresa still in his lap. As if there was some silent signal, everyone hushed and gave Ethan and Theresa space. His grandmother turned her attention to her fire building. Mom, Keisha, and Ethan's mother went into the kitchen and started making dish-rattling, clean-up sounds. The snake's body was still now, and Dad was digging a hole—I guess to bury it.

I stood, uncertain where I should go, unable to take my eyes off Ethan and Theresa. She lay quiet, eyes closed, still curled against him. Ethan caught my eye and patted the chair next to him. As I approached, he pulled my chair flush against his. I quietly collapsed into it.

Here we were in the same spot we'd been only minutes earlier, but so much had changed. I caressed his arm that lay on the arm-rests of our pushed-together chairs. The same arms that minutes ago had been so strong and courageous were now gentle and comforting. He shifted and put his arm around my shoulders and pulled me closer. I rested my head against the front of his shoulder, placed one palm on his chest, and felt the steady beat of his heart.

He kissed the top of my head and then leaned his cheek against my hair. "Everything is all right now. We'll sit here until we feel better." His grandmother must have plugged in her Christmas lights because we were suddenly surrounded by red, green and blue lights.

Theresa opened her eyes and gazed straight into mine. I had smiled at Ethan's words, but her sad expression flattened the budding relief I was feeling.

With one palm still on Ethan's chest, I rested my other hand on Theresa's knees. "It's okay, Theresa. The snake is gone. It can't hurt anyone now. Ethan saved us. He was so fast and brave and smart. Everyone is okay."

I hoped my words would bring a smile, but instead two giant tears flowed from her eyes. She didn't make a sound, but her chest heaved up and down.

Her tears made my own eyes well. "Theresa, what's wrong? Are you still scared?"

She shook her head.

From somewhere in the house, "Oh Holy Night" started playing.

Ethan squeezed my shoulder. And he began to speak to Theresa in a tone that reached into my heart and made me realize when a man's deep, strong voice becomes gentle and comforting, it carries a magical strength. His words touched the deepest part of me. "Theresa, you feel sad that I killed the snake. It hurts you to see things die." It was in that moment that I fully absorbed the dimensions of Ethan.

Theresa gasped a sob, gave one jerky nod, and pressed herself closer to Ethan.

His gentle voice crooned. "It's okay that you feel sad. I feel sad, too. If I would have had a way to capture it and take it to a wilderness, I would have done it. But I killed it because I was afraid if I let it go free, it might have returned when I wasn't here, and it could have bitten you or Keisha."

She reached both her arms around his neck and wept hard, loud sobs.

Patiently, for at least half an hour, he assured and comforted her. Until finally the tension flowed out of her body, her arms released his neck and collapsed onto her chest.

The Christmas music from inside the house continued to drift out, and the colorful lights blinked into the darkness around us. The night air grew a little cooler, but close to his chest with his arm around my shoulders, I felt warm. I loved the earthy scent of him—his body, his breath. I loved the steady beating of his heart beneath my palm. I loved the sound of his voice and the kindness in his words. I loved that he could be frighteningly brutal when it came to protecting his loved ones but heart-tugging tender when it came to comforting those same loved ones. I loved him.

And I will love him forever.

BOOKS BY BRENDA

Polarity in Motion by Brenda Vicars

Polarity in Love (to be published 2019) by Brenda Vicars

Faking Lucky by Q. D. Purdu (penname for Brenda Vicars)

The Light we Found by Q. D. Purdu (Penname for Brenda Vicars)

ABOUT BRENDA

Brenda Vicars has worked in Texas public education for many years. Her jobs have included teaching, serving as a principal, and directing student support programs. For three years, she also taught college English to prison inmates.

She entered education because she felt called to teach, but her students taught her the biggest lesson: the playing field is not even for all kids. Through her work, she became increasingly compelled to bring their unheard voices to the page. The heartbeat of her fiction emanates from the courage and resiliency of her students.

GET IN TOUCH:

https://twitter.com/BrendaVicars
www.brendavicars.com
https://www.facebook.com/brenda.vicars.12
https://www.facebook.com/Brenda-Vicars-509794745822839/

Yuletide Homicide: A Liz Boyle Short Mystery

BY KATE BIRDSALL

It's two-thirty a.m. and still snowing when I climb down from my Cleveland Police Explorer. The wind from Lake Erie blasts ice into my face as I duck under the yellow crime-scene tape. "You caught the Edgewater snowman, Boyle?" a uniform asks as he hands me a clipboard..

"Yup. Lucky me." This isn't my regular shift, and a straightforward homicide isn't my usual kind of case. I volunteered to take Christmas Eve overnight because everyone else has family shit to do. I would just as soon not spend the holiday with mine. That's just how it goes.

I sign in then glance around. There's a city salt truck stopped in the middle of Detroit Boulevard, a group of unis surrounding what appears to be a frozen Santa atop a snow bank, and a gaggle of other unis working to block the road. "Castor here?" Rick Castor, head of homicide, called me to the scene.

He nods. "By the body. I sure as shit hope the news doesn't show up. Dead Santa makes for sad kids."

"Indeed." I catch Castor's eye, and he ambles over my way.

"Someone made the naughty list."

I laugh. "Did you just make a joke?" Castor has never been one for humor.

"I did. I mean, you kind of have to, right? It's a dead Santa. Here's what we know: round two o'clock, salt truck was following the plow. Driver saw Mr. Claus's torso sticking out of that snowbank. Looks like the plow churned it up or something." He shakes his head. "This city is something else."

I nod and pull my hat down over my ears. "Why are we thinking homicide?"

"Gunshot wound to the chest."

"That'll do it. Any witnesses other than salt guy?"

"Nope. This one's going on the shelf."

"We might figure it out. I'm on it." It would be a Christmas miracle.

"Right. You working solo?"

"It's Christmas."

He grins. "Happy effing holidays, Boyle. Keep me posted."

Four hours later, just as we're clearing the scene to reopen Detroit Boulevard for holiday traffic, I get a text from my partner, Tom Goran: *You working?*

Instead of replying, I call him. "Of course I'm working. What else would I be doing?"

"Merry Christmas to you too."

"Why are you calling me?" We love each other like siblings, but I'm cold and grumpy and need about sixteen shots of espresso if I'm going to keep working this case.

"I figured you might want some help."

"Don't you have Christmas stuff?"

"Yeah, but I've got a couple of hours. What's happening? I can help you over the phone."

"I just rolled my eyes at you, Goran. I caught the dead Santa up by Edgewater. It's cold as shit out here. My hands are numb—"

"Are you wearing gloves and your poofy coat?"

"Just rolled my eyes *again*. Of course." I fill him in. "ME's office just took the body. It's gotta thaw before the postmortem, and that could take a couple of days. We think he died sometime late on the twenty-third. And here's the kicker—we found one of those red money buckets not far from the body. I'm thinking he was a bell-ringer. No ID."

"Money still inside?"

"Yup." I wave at a uniform as I climb into my truck. I start it and crank the heat up. "There's not a lot of blood, so it's clear that Santa died somewhere other than where the salt guy found his body."

"Hmmm. You checking with the Salvation Army?"

"Of course. Right now, I'm heading back to do paperwork. Hoping to get out of there in time to do Christmas." I turn the headlights on and shift into Drive.

"Family?"

"Hell no. Christopher still isn't talking to me, and I can't deal with my mom. I've got plans with Josh and Jacob and Cora. The J's are having a get-together." I head east on Detroit.

"You and Cora going together?"

"I'm picking her up, yeah."

"Not what I meant. You two have fun. And call me if you need my massive and methodical brain."

I laugh. "Merry Christmas, Tom. Love to Vera and the girls."

"Merry Christmas, Boyle. Stay out of trouble."

I get back to the squad room, make a pot of coffee, and start the crime board before calling the Salvation Army. When I've been on hold with the national office for sixteen minutes I thumb through the murder books on my desk, considering the calls I need to make next week. That double-murder in Little Italy… I grab my notebook and write myself a reminder. *Interview woman at laundromat.* Police work doesn't take holiday time, and those cases are more urgent than I want them to be.

Seven minutes later, someone answers the phone. "Salvation Army Cuyahoga County, this is Brenna," the woman says. She sounds bored and out of breath at the same time.

"Hi, Brenna. This is Detective Elizabeth Boyle with Cleveland Homicide. I have a couple of questions."

"Is this going to take a while? I have somewhere to be."

"It shouldn't take long. Can you tell me whether your employees sign in and out for their shifts?"

"Yeah, we use a phone app."

"Can you verify that all of your employees working in the past three days are accounted for?"

"Yeah, I know they are, because I just did stupid payroll. They're all here. And they're done for the season now, so they're getting their last checks next week. I can't believe I came in on Christmas for this."

Spoken like a woman who truly believes in the spirit of giving. "And you know for sure that everyone working in the past three days clocked out for their shifts?"

"I just said that."

I squeeze the bridge of my nose. "Do you have anyone who routinely dresses as Santa for the job?"

"What? Dresses as Santa? Yeah, a lot of 'em do. I don't keep a list."

"Okay, Brenna. Thanks for your time. Will you call me if you think of anything or if someone doesn't pick up a check?"

"It's all direct deposit, but yeah, whatever."

I give her my number and thank her again for her patience. I probably sound as sarcastic as I feel.

I finish my reports, email them to Castor, then head home to feed the cat and attempt a nap. Josh texts me to remind me that the get-together starts at five, so I let Cora to know I'll pick her up at six. It's always good to be fashionably late to fashionable people's parties.

Cora and I used to date before our relationship ended in a decidedly dramatic way. I admit to screwing it up—I was drinking too much, not taking the antidepressants it turns out I need, and getting too immersed in work. After I tried to atone for my sins a while back, she decided to be friends with me for reasons I'll never understand. I'm not the most lovable person in the world.

I keep my word and pick her up at six o'clock.

"Are you sure it's casual?" she asks. She looks fantastic in leggings, a long sweater, and tall boots. In true Cora style, she has the sweater pushed up to show her tattoos, full sleeves on both arms, and her hair is in a messy bun, revealing the top of her neck and back piece.

"Of course it is, and you look great. It's just people sitting around and talking about smart things. I'm surprised I was invited. Were you planning on wearing a cocktail dress?" We chuckle together as she hems and haws before running upstairs to grab a striped scarf, coming back down, and making an ostentatious show of draping it around her neck. We laugh louder.

I watch her apply lipstick. *You have the most beautiful mouth in the universe.*

"Go warm up the car. I know it takes forever to get warm."

I do as I'm told. As I'm waiting for her, a text message from Castor comes through: *Got reports. Thanks. Merry Christmas.*

I reply in kind. Cora climbs into my VW—which is becoming something of a clunker these days—and puts on her seatbelt. "You caught a case. You have that look."

I fill her in. She's a detective with the police department in neighboring Cleveland Heights, so we talk shop sometimes.

"That's strange," she says. "Do you think he's a bell-ringer, or do you think he might be the guy who's been *stealing* from the bell-ringers?"

I brake behind a big black SUV. "Wait, what? The super-helpful woman at Salvation Army didn't say anything about that."

She sighs. "Those people are impossible. Yeah, some guy in a Santa suit has been attacking bell-ringers all season. He hits them with pepper spray then steals their buckets. It's a serial thing."

The light turns, and I laugh as I accelerate around the SUV. "I'm sorry. It's not funny. Just the image—"

"—of a guy in a Santa suit stealing from other guys in Santa suits? It's funny. I know. Fortunately, no one has been hurt too badly until now."

"Well, this one is dead, and the Salvation Army says they're all accounted for."

"I'll give you my case notes tomorrow. The guy is about five-ten, two-fifty. Surveillance video makes it look like his hair and beard are real—looks like Santa."

"It totally figures that you would have notes and that he would target Cleveland Heights."

"Ha ha. It's not just us. The guy has been working his way across the whole east side since Thanksgiving, and most of the suburban departments are looking for him. Don't you watch the news?"

I narrow my eyes. "Not anymore, no, not unless I have to. The guy you just described matches my vic's description. Once he unthaws, we'll know more."

She shudders.

We make small talk for a few minutes with Josh and his partner, Jacob, before Jacob introduces Cora to the others. Josh is a pediatric oncologist, Jacob is an attorney, all of their friends are professional types, and I'm a little rough around the edges. Cora comes off as far more regal than I do. I look down at my black jeans, beat-up boots, and worn sweater. I might need to invest in both a new car and a new personal wardrobe. *You can take the kid out of the nineties, but you can't take the nineties out of the kid.*

At some point after dinner, Josh pulls me into the kitchen. "I can't believe you actually made it," he says, pushing his rimless glasses up on his nose.

"What else would I be doing?" I gesture at my empty wine glass.

"Working, drinking whisky, or figuring out a way to avoid seeing Margaret."

I point at him with my free hand. "Avoiding seeing Mom, check. Drinking, check—though it's wine and not bourbon, which we both know isn't just 'whisky,' and I can't have too much 'cause I'm driving. Working, also check. I worked all night and this morning. Dead Santa. Don't ask."

He laughs. "Come on. Tell me about the dead Santa. That's darkly hilarious."

"It's a dead end. I told you not to ask." I fill him in anyway, complete with the part about a guy in a Santa suit robbing bell-ringers.

He frowns. "What is wrong with people?"

"Desperation drives people to do all kinds of heinous shit."

"God, can you imagine kids finding out about that? Talk about ruining Christmas." He slides the cork out of the wine and decants it. "Maybe it's not funny after all."

I nod. "Let's hope good old mom and dad didn't turn on the news while little Johnnie and Janey were opening presents."

"So. Cora." He wiggles his eyebrows.

"Uh huh. What about her?"

"What's going on with you two?" He makes a hurry-up gesture.

"Who?"

He puts his hands on his hips. "Don't do that, Liz."

"I still care about her. You wouldn't believe me if I told you how much." I lean back against the counter.

"You know you just said that out loud, right? And that you're actually standing in my kitchen with me on Christmas? And that you're behaving really well these days?"

I feel my face turn red. "Yeah, well, I'm trying."

"The therapy is helping. It's obvious."

He doesn't know about the anti-depressants. I think about my shrink in her swanky office up by the lake.

"Are you back together?"

"No."

"Are you moving on?"

"No."

"Why not?"

"Something is wrong with me."

"Girl, I've known that for over thirty-five years. Hand me your glass." I oblige, and he fills it. "Have you told her?"

"Told her what?" I sip the Grenache. "This is fantastic."

"That you still love her, you jerk." He rolls his eyes, fills his glass, and sets the carafe on the counter.

"I can't. I'm scared."

"Of what? Jesus, Liz, live a little. She obviously still wants to hang out with you, even though you're a major pain in the ass." He smiles and puts an arm around me. "But I still love you, even when you're impossible. And I *really* love you when you're on good behavior."

"But what if—" I let my voice trail off. *What if she only puts up with me, even as a friend, because she feels bad for me?*

"What if what? What if she doesn't want to get back together? What if she does?" He releases my shoulders. "You need to let yourself be a human being. I can think of nothing more depressing in this world than never loving anyone."

"I love Ivan." I take a big sip of wine.

"He's a *cat*."

"I love my brother, at least for the most part."

"Do you love me?"

"Of course."

"Tell me."

"I love you, Josh." It's my turn to roll my eyes.

"Was that so hard?"

I shake my head.

"Listen, Liz. Here it is. You need to tell Cora what you just told me. I'm serious. We're all too old for this. If you want to be with her, make it happen."

"I will."

"You'll what?"

"I'll be an adult and share my feelings. I'll put words to them or whatever the hell you're telling me to do."

"Pretty sure you learned that in therapy." He sings "therapy" in a way that makes me laugh.

I hear someone stifle a chuckle from behind the door, and Cora pushes through, pretending she hasn't been standing there the whole time. "I'm empty," she says, waving her wine glass at us.

Josh gives me an admonishing stare then grins at her. "What would you like, my dear?" He puts his arm around her casually and leads her to the wine rack.

I chuckle. "Leave her alone, Josh."

"She's not my type," he says. Then he turns to face Cora. "I mean no offense. You would *definitely* be my type if I were single and even remotely interested in your gender." He grins as she laughs. "I'm serious," he said. "You really are stunning, and you're smart as hell, or she wouldn't still be pining away for you. Then again, if you were really that smart, you probably wouldn't be here with her." He winks at me.

"Thank you, Josh, for that lovely intervention." I feel myself blush. Cora and I exchange a glance. *We really are too old for this. Cora turns forty in April.*

"How about this one?" She slides a good Tempranillo out of the rack. "I love Spanish wine."

He takes the bottle from her. "You have good taste in everything but careers and women, it would seem." He can't help himself.

She laughs. "The job is just a job, and I have good taste in women, too."

His light-brown eyes search hers from behind his glasses before he peels the foil off the top of the bottle. "Watch yourself, girl. Spending time with Liz is like playing with matches." He tilts his head in my direction.

I feel my eyebrows come together in the middle of my face. "Okay, guys, this is getting weird. I'm standing right here."

They both turn to face me. "And how nice it is to have you here," Cora says.

"I'm going to the bathroom." I turn to leave.

"She still cares a lot about you," I hear Josh telling her as he slides the cork out of the wine. I resist the urge to listen at the door.

We leave around ten and decide to celebrate the rest of the evening at my apartment. Once inside, I toss Cora a pair of snow boots. "Put those on. I'll get the wine." I hesitate on my way out of the room but leave to fetch a bottle and an opener. "Will you be warm enough to walk somewhere with me?"

She looks conflicted but nods. "Sure. Lead the way."

I pull an old Cleveland Browns hat down over my ears then hand her my plain black watch cap.

As we trudge through the snow to Cumberland park, about a twelve-minute walk from my building, I open the wine. "Swings," I say, swigging from the bottle. I hand it to her.

"Oh, all we need is public intox," she replies, but she takes a sip anyway. "Nothing like a couple of detectives getting busted on Christmas."

We laugh. "Oh, right, we are in bored-in-Heights-ville." It's a joke that CDP makes all the time about Cleveland Heights, and Cora is a good sport.

"I was off last night," she reminds me. "Were you?"

"Touché." I lead her to a swing set, where we have a contest to see who can go higher. I win because Cora is worried about flipping over the bar, but then she jumps off of the swing, flies through the air, and lands on her feet like a cat. "I stuck the landing!" she shouts, laughing wildly.

We make a couple of snow angels, and I'm in awe when she kisses me deeply. "Let's go," I whisper. "The snow. We're wet." I pull her up, and we tromp arm-in-arm through the snow and back to my apartment, where we make love then fall asleep together.

I'm awakened by the sound of my phone. I scrub my hand over my face, remove Cora's arm from around my waist, and squint at the screen. Castor. I slide out of bed, careful not to wake her, and take the call in the kitchen.

"You're never gonna believe this," he says.

I yawn and fill the coffee maker with water. "Believe what?"

"He turned himself in. Our frozen-Santa perp. He came in two hours ago and spilled it all."

I fill the basket with coffee. "No shit. Really? Let me guess. Just hear me out."

"Go for it. You get it right, I'm buying rounds when you're back on."

"I'm on tomorrow. I think our vic was robbing local bell-ringers. One of the guys he robbed got pissed. He followed the robber without involving the police, because the suburbs couldn't seem to catch him, and shot him. They were over on the west side because the vic, also the thief, lives over there and was targeting the east side to throw us off."

Castor whistles. He doesn't know what I know about the Santa robber or that I'm just spinning a story—I don't have Cora's notes yet. *Could it be this easy? Don't think about the other cases. Don't think about whatever you'll catch after your days off. Let it be easy, because it never is.*

I keep going. "Our perp got the vic into his car somehow, shot him, then dumped him up on Detroit. He cleaned up the mess, went home to his family, and felt guilty."

"How about motive?" Castor asks.

"Hmm. That's harder. Whose motive?"

"The thief."

"The thief used to work for the Salvation Army but was let go for some reason. He needed money to buy a present for his grandkid."

"You are so, so close," he replies. "Damn, Boyle, are you sure you don't want to come work for me?"

I chuckle. "What was off?"

"The thief's motive. We don't know it yet, and we may not ever. We're notifying next of kin today."

I sigh. "Want me to come in and take care of it?"

"Nah. Good work, Boyle. I really appreciate you covering the desk. Beer's on me. Seriously."

I can't bring myself to tell him that Cora basically solved the case. "Thanks, Castor. Have a good one."

"Ten-four."

We end the call just as the coffee maker brews enough for two cups. I dump a lot of cream in mine and a dash into Cora's before filling the mugs and taking them to the bedroom.

I'll have to tell her she was right.

I have a lot of things to say to her.

BOOKS BY KATE

The Flats: A Liz Boyle Mystery

ABOUT KATE

Kate Birdsall was born in the heart of the Rust Belt and harbors a hesitant affinity for its grit. She's an existentialist who writes both short and long fiction, and she plays a variety of loud instruments. She lives in Michigan's capital city with her partner and at least one too many four-legged creatures.

GET IN TOUCH:

Website: www.katebirdsall.com
Facebook: www.facebook.com/katebirdsallauthor
Instagram: www.instagram.com/punkrockmysterywriter/?hl=en
Twitter: @KEBirdsall

A Crazy Christmas

BY KELLY STONE GAMBLE

'm standing on Grams' porch with a hammer in one hand and an arm full of tangled Christmas lights in the other, wishing I could just set the large oak in the front yard on fire instead of decorating it.

"What are you waiting for? Straighten those out so we can see why the hell they don't work, then we can get this over with." Roland crumples up his empty can of PBR, throws it in Grams' yard, and grabs another one from the half-gone twelve pack next to him.

"This would have been easier if you'd have been here five hours ago like you said you would," I say. I bite my lip as soon as the words leave my mouth.

It's Christmas Eve, and Roland dropped me off this morning so I could help Grams cook. He said he'd be back by noon. I wasn't going to mention it because he left with a pocketful of money and I'm kind of hoping he's been out trying to find me a pair of those black and green Lucchese ostrich boots I've been hinting that I want. Hell, I showed him the picture four times and left it on the seat of his truck this morning. He'd have to be dumber than a slug eating salt to miss that.

"It would have been easier if your looney Grandma paid someone to put the damn lights up a week ago. And besides, I had shit to do," he says. Roland always has shit to do.

"Grams says it's bad luck to put the lights up early," I say as I try to find the end of the string of lights.

Roland stands up and stretches while I continue to try to unwrap the lights. It seems like I'm tying them in knots instead of untangling them. I wish I hadn't taken my pills this morning; they always make me fuzzy, and it sure would have been easier to do this if I could think straight. But it's Christmas Eve, and the last thing I want is for Roland to start in on me about not taking my pills. He says they keep me from doing crazy shit but I'm pretty sure I'm capable of that with or without the pills. He just doesn't know that.

"Here we go." Roland laughs and motions toward the street. Clay, Roland's brother, is parking his truck in front of Grams' house. Even from here, I can see that the cab of his truck is loaded with presents—the red, green, and silver paper and bows peek over the passenger door and block my view of him in the truck. He gets out carrying three packages and smiles as he walks toward us.

"Merry Christmas," he says.

I can't help but smile at Clay. He's the quiet one of the two brothers, and unlike most people in town, is always nice to me. I don't see him much since Roland moved us to the shack on the outside of town, but when I do, it's like he's excited to see me. *Me*. Not Roland. He can't stand his brother, and the feeling is mutual. "Who are all the presents for?" I ask and nod toward the truck.

"Shaylene," he says. "She and her mom open presents at midnight, so I thought it would be easier to load—"

"Whatever," Roland says. Shaylene is Clay's adopted daughter, and I don't think Roland considers her to be a real niece. "Say, you should be familiar with things that are sparkly. Why don't you help Cass with these lights?" Roland thinks Clay is gay because he never seems to have a girlfriend. I think he just hasn't found anyone he wants to hang out with for very long.

Clay squints at Roland. Then he takes the lights from me and hands me the presents. "Not a problem."

Roland's phone dings and he looks at it and smiles. "I'll be back," he says.

"Wait! Where are you going?" I say.

"Tina says there's some trouble at the club and I'm the one she calls when there's a problem." He thumps me on the forehead with two fingers. "And besides, I don't need to tell you where I'm goin', remember?" Roland is the head bouncer at Fat Tina's strip joint on the outside of town. It seems like she always has "trouble" out there.

"Dinner is at seven and then we open presents. Don't be late!" I scream at his back as he walks toward his truck, swinging the rest of his twelve-pack beside him.

Clay shakes his head and I hear him mumble, "What a piece of work." Then he turns to me and the big smile is back. "Don't worry about him. Go help your grandmother with dinner and I'll get these lights put up. The big tree in front, right?"

"Yeah," I say as I watch Roland's pickup turn left at the corner on Eighteenth Street. I know Tina's is to the right.

Last year, Grams bought me *How the Grinch Stole Christmas!* on DVD—the original one, not the new one where the Grinch is an empty-headed flake instead of a pissed-off sadist in need of a good ass whoopin'—and I'm watching it for the second time after eating too much dinner and way too much butterscotch bread pudding. And cherry cobbler. And pecan pie.

"Maybe we should go ahead and open our presents," Grams says. It's almost ten o'clock and no Roland. Grams doesn't seem surprised, Clay looks pissed, and I'm feeling a lot like Max the dog, forced to do all the real work while the Grinch has his fun.

"Good idea," Clay says. He hands Grams a small red box with a silver bow and she tears into it like a raccoon at the city dump.

Grams pulls out a cheap, beaded necklace and gasps like it's the crown jewels. "Oh, my stars! How did you think of this?"

"I saw that picture you have of Jim Morrison in the bathroom and thought that necklace looked like it meant something," he says.

"It does!" She fingers the beads, pointing out the colors. "The black beads mean he was mysterious, the green and brown mean he was down-to-earth, and the white is his spirituality." Grams is a bit of a Doors fan and has pictures of the lead singer all over her house. She's also into people's auras and colors and things like that, so it isn't surprising that she knows what all the beads mean.

She goes to the bathroom and returns with the picture of the bare chested-dude off the wall, so she can compare the necklaces. I shake my head.

I give her my present, a new deck of tarot cards to replace the ones I accidentally spilled Kool-Aid on a few weeks ago. Even though I know she has at least five other decks, again, she acts like it's the greatest thing since cracked pepper. It doesn't take much to please Grams.

I give Clay a T-shirt that says "I've Got Worms" because I know he has a bunch of little huts in his backyard full of worms that he sells for bait. Grams gives him a burlap sack of something that smells like old hay and cherries that he's supposed to put in his bedroom to help his love life. Clay is another one that's easy to please.

As they hand me their gifts, I hear a car door slam and jump up. "It's about time," I say. I open the door and right in front of the big tree that Clay decorated with lights, I see Benny Cloud, the Deacon Chief of Police. He's standing over Roland, who is barfing his guts out.

"What the hell did you do to him, Benny?" I say.

"I saved him from a DWI, is what I did. The truck is at the station. Have him pick it up in the morning when he's sober," he says.

Clay passes me on the porch, hauls Roland up, and drags him toward the house. I focus on Benny. "If you'd of been doing your job and taking care of the trouble out at Fat Tina's, he wouldn't have had to drive at all!" I say. I pick up one of the empty beer cans in the yard and throw it at Benny's truck, then plant my feet and put my hands on my hips, daring him to say something about it.

He grunts like an old bear. "Tina's is closed today. It's Christmas Eve," he says. He nods to Grams and Clay, shakes his head at me, then crawls back in his Tahoe.

"Merry Christmas!" Roland slurs as Clay drops him on the couch. He digs in his pocket and pulls out a black votive candle and hands it to Grams. "Here's another candle. I'm sure you think it means something," he says.

She takes it and stares at it. "Yes, black is to fight off negative energy."

"You might want to light that one," Clay says.

"Oh, you're a funny guy," Roland says. He digs in another pocket and throws a handful of pink condoms at Clay, all branded with Fat Tina's logo. "Merry Christmas, brother, maybe you can get laid now."

I'm standing there, waiting, but Roland doesn't even look at me. You'd think after all these years, I'd realize that he isn't ever going to change. He used to be such a great guy; always thought about me first, always wanted to make sure I was happy. But as the years have gone by, he's become a real ass.

I sit down in front of the large box Clay had given me and finger the large gold bow on top. "Open it," Clay says.

Slowly, I release the pieces of tape, one by one, and unfold the paper: a pair of black Laredo boots with green roses embroidered on the sides. "They aren't ostrich, but I thought they were pretty," he says. "Merry Christmas."

They aren't the boots I wanted, but Clay's right, they are pretty, and I haven't had a new pair of boots in a long time. I put them on and feel like Cinderella, walking around the living room in my green and black Laredo slippers. Roland is passed out, or just not paying any attention, and I don't even care. The doorbell rings, which wakes up Roland, and he staggers to the door saying, "I'll get rid of them."

It's Benny Cloud. Again. He hands Roland a long package wrapped in brown paper. "You left this in the Tahoe."

Roland immediately hands it to me. "Here. Now you can help me with some of the yard work instead of sittin' on the couch all day watching Jerry Springer."

I unwrap the package and hold up a long-handled spade. "What the hell do I need a shovel for?"

He stumbles through the living room, headed for the bathroom, and mumbles, "You'll think of something."

Grams lights her new black candle and sits it on the coffee table. I hear Roland throwing up in the bathroom, and hope to hell he made it to the commode. I hold the shovel up and nod my head. Yeah, I'll think of something.

GRAMS' BUTTERSCOTCH BREAD PUDDING

Ingredients:

6 day-old hamburger buns, torn into small pieces- For protection, peace, and love

1 Tablespoon of cinnamon- For prosperity

1 teaspoon of ginger- For good health

1 teaspoon of nutmeg- For good luck

2 teaspoons of vanilla extract- For love

1 cup of butterscotch chips- For happiness

1/2 cup of finely chopped pecans- For money

2 cups of brown sugar-For a little magic

4 cups of milk

1/2 cup of butter, melted

3 eggs, beaten

Directions:

1. Preheat oven to 350 degrees F (175 degrees C). Butter a 9x13 inch baking dish.

2. In a large bowl, combine all of the ingredients, making sure you stir in a clockwise motion to bring about health, success, and a harmonious life. Pour into prepared pan.

3. Bake in preheated oven 1 hour, until nearly set (It should wiggle). Serve warm or cold.

BOOKS BY KELLY

They Call Me Crazy

Call Me Daddy

Call Me Cass

ABOUT KELLY

Kelly Stone Gamble is the author of USA TODAY bestseller *They Call Me Crazy*, *Call Me Daddy*, and *Call Me Cass*. Since 2000, she has had over fifty articles, essays and short stories published in anthologies, magazines and journals including:

- Red Earth Review
- Tower Journal
- Family Fun
- Family Digest
- Message Magazine
- Chicken Soup for the Soul

Her fiction has won awards from Writers Weekly, Writers Courtyard, Women on Writing and the Ground Zero Literary Project.

She is an Instructor for Southeastern Oklahoma State University and lives in Henderson, Nevada and Idabel, Oklahoma.

GET IN TOUCH

www.kstonegamble.com
https://www.goodreads.com/author/show/9230926.Kelly_Stone_Gamble
https://redadeptpublishing.com/team/kelly-stone-gamble/
https://www.facebook.com/KStoneGamble/

Rowen's Gift

BY MICHAEL MEYERHOFER

I know you won't believe a word of this, but I'm going to tell you anyway. Not that I blame you for thinking I'm a liar, you understand. These days, everyone from the Lotus Isles to Dhargoth seems to have a story about how they knew Rowen Locke. Some claim they fought beside him in the war, that they were so close when he battled Fadarah that they could actually feel the heat wafting off that burning sword of his.

Others like to keep their lies more believable. They say they met him back in the early days, long before he was a hero, when he was just another grubby sellsword sleeping in ditches. *Oh, you should have seen him,* they say. *Even then, he spoke in poetry. Even then, men would have followed him into a dragon's maw, if he'd asked!* Usually, they throw in a bit about how they saved his life, just for good measure. But men lie as easily as the stars shine, and I guess I'm no different.

This time, though, I'm going to give the truth a try. See, I know what's waiting for me when the dawn splashes red through these iron bars, and I don't expect anything I say to change that. But I already paid what few coins I had left to the priest who's writing this down, so here goes.

I knew Rowen Locke from when we were children in Lyos. Did I say Lyos? The Dark Quarter, more like it. That's what they call the slums where we grew up… though nowadays, thanks to the storytellers, you probably already knew that. Strange to hear the Dark Quarter talked about like it's some kind of romantic place where thieves get together and talk philosophy. Personally, when I think about that place, I mostly just remember the smell of burnt dog.

Anyway, I was an orphan there, same as Locke. That's not to say we were friends. I'm sure he doesn't even remember me. See, we barely ever spoke. In a place like the Dark Quarter, if you want to live long, best you join up with one of the gangs—the Bloody Asps, the Crazy Knifemen, maybe even the Skull-Breakers, if blunt force is more your thing. Only Locke was different. His older brother, Kayden—gods, there was a mean one!—he scrapped alongside the gangs, same as me, same as everyone. But Rowen Locke kept out of it as much as he could.

It's not that he was soft-hearted. Sweet goddess, I once saw him walk into a tavern—calm as falling snow—pluck a knife from a man's belt, and use it to open that same man's stomach. Repayment for a crime inflicted on some of the local children, the kind of crime even the gangs won't stand for. They say he got permission from them before he did the deed, though they might have just said that after, to save face.

Anyway, when it was done, nobody said a word. I don't think anybody could believe it. All you heard was that bastard howling. Everybody thought Locke would leave him like that, leave him to die slow and painful. Instead, Locke bent in and finished him off—still placid as the Wintersea—then dropped the knife and walked out. Oh, and in case I wasn't clear, Locke wasn't no grown man when he did it. The man he killed was big as a tree, sure, but I doubt Locke had more than twelve years on his bones at the time. I wasn't much older.

Thing I want to add, though, is that after it was done and they hauled out the dead man to rot—I don't even remember his name—everybody took to laughing and cheering, like it was some grand joke. I laughed, too. Only I saw Locke later, in an alley overgrown with weeds and sprinkled with dog-bones, crying like a kid who'd had his toy stolen. That brother of his was looming over him. When Kayden saw me, he chased me off. But I could tell I'd interrupted him yelling at little Rowen, hitting him, telling him to toughen up. I can't blame him. In the Dark Quarter, tears are a waste of water.

I said before that Locke and I weren't friends. Truth is, I hated him. Oh, he was tough, and that ain't nothing, but I was still living in the Dark Quarter a stack of years later when he came back and joined the Red Watch. Maybe you think the Red Watch is just the city guard, pretty much the same as any other city big enough to host soldiers. But for a slum-dweller, joining the Red Watch is like turning traitor. When I saw him come back after all those years, dressed in that damn scarlet uniform, part of me wanted to sneak up and do to him what he'd done to that child-raper all those years before.

It wasn't just that he'd turned traitor, though. See, for years, we'd all been hearing how Rowen Locke sailed off to the Lotus Isles to become a Knight, same as his brother. That he actually had a chance for a life outside of gangs and graverobbing. Only here he was, face blushing the same color as his tabard, and what happened was obvious: he'd failed.

That's the part the storytellers forget. Before Rowen Locke became a hero, he tried to become a Knight, and they turned him away. His brother made it, sure, but Kayden got himself killed, and when it came Rowen's turn to earn his armor, he didn't meet the measure. So here he was, right back in the slums he'd tried so hard to escape. Only now, he was on the wrong side.

Sweet goddess, I despised him for that. *If I'd had a chance like he did,* I told myself, *ain't no man or demon that would stop me.* Night after night, I thought about killing him, as a kind of revenge for letting us down. Maybe given more time and enough ale, I might have actually tried something. Only if you already know Locke's story, you know what happened next: the witch he saved, the battles he fought, how he actually united the Red Watch with the gangs from the Dark Quarter and did things you'd have to see to believe.

Only I wasn't there to see it. I had sense enough to get out of Lyos as soon as I sensed trouble brewing. I had friends in the Skull-Breakers who wanted me to stay, but I wouldn't have it. Now, some of those friends are rich heroes living up in the city proper, while others are living in the ground. So I guess you could say I missed my chance to be a hero. But I kept my organs in the right places, and that ain't nothing, either.

For years after that, I wandered, taking work where I could—and not the kind of work that good men brag about. I tried to forget all about Locke and what might have been, if I'd stayed. Only I kept hearing his name mentioned in taverns, in songs that made my skin crawl and my knuckles turn white. I knew those minstrels would never sing about me. I'd grown up in the same swill as Locke, done most of the same sins, only he was the hero. I was no one. And I'd never be anything else.

Finally, I couldn't take it anymore. One night, in some nameless little pig-town on the Simurgh Plains, I grabbed one of those minstrels—a young man with a face like a woman's—and beat him within an inch of his life. Only that didn't make me feel much better. And anyway, after that, I had to run. Turns out that minstrel's family had a mind for revenge, his pretty face ruined and all, plus enough coins to hire a couple throat-slitters to come after me.

Ah, but I can see by the priest's grimace, the priest who's been writing all this down like a good little vessel for the goddess's boundless love, that he doesn't care much for my story. Don't worry, Father. There isn't much left. I can already see a little orange on the horizon and I'm sure they'll be coming for me before long. So I'll just wrap this up and let you be on your way.

By and by, I got away from the throat-slitters. It was winter so maybe the blizzards changed their minds. Or maybe they got caught up in the war, all those armies surging back and forth. But it doesn't matter because I still ended up in a jail in Phaegos. Don't ask me why. I woke up in chains, with a headache that said there was no point trying to remember how I'd gotten there. All I knew was what the jailor told me: that they were going to hang me as soon as the blizzard let up, along with a dozen or so other lads and ladies who'd offended whoever was in charge.

Believe it or not, it was the Feast of Tier'Gothma. I only knew that because the jailor told us. Gods, I wish he hadn't. I've never had much use for holy days, leastwise ones that call upon you to give your loved ones presents and tell them you can't live without them. I don't know. Maybe I'd feel different, if I actually had loved ones. But it's an awful thing, to face your death on a day when you're supposed to be celebrating life.

Only that didn't happen—the hanging, I mean. Because the gods have a brutish sense of humor, there I was—scared out of my mind, praying the snows wouldn't let up, praying for another day, another hour—when word came that Locke's army was heading this way. Locke's *army!* Turns out he was a gods-damned general now. And like you'd expect, he was busy hunting somebody who needed to be robbed of life even more than I did. What's more, every city that wanted to earn themselves a verse in future songs was already donating soldiers to his cause. But the governor of Phaegos didn't want to risk his own men, so he gathered us condemned and gave us a choice: swing from the gallows like rotten apples, or put on uniforms and go fight demons or some such nonsense.

Your Feastday gift, he called it. The bastard.

Well, I said I'd go. I would have said anything. I planned to run as soon as I got the chance. Only once we were free, the great Rowen Locke himself came to talk to us. Gods, I hardly recognized him—all that silk and armor, plus a few fresh scars. But it was still the same face under all that kingsteel and polish. He gave us a fine speech, right there in the snow: told us that despite what we'd agreed to, he wouldn't keep us against our will. He said that mercy was a choice, not a gift. He said we could go if we wanted. He wouldn't stop us.

Only nobody left. His pretty words convinced everybody to stay and fight, to rise above their lot, to become heroes. Everybody but me.

Like I said, I don't think he even recognized me. And he never saw me again. Come morning, I was already miles away. After a while, my anger cooled, but by then it was too late. The war was over. The gods had given me a second chance, the only gift I've ever been given, and I wasted it. Do you have any idea what that kind of knowledge does to a man? Is it any wonder I did what I did?

No, Father, don't answer. I already know what you're going to say. You can keep your sermons and incantations to yourself. And don't think for a second that I don't get the irony here. A year since I ran from Locke. A year, almost to the day. Only this time, I doubt the great general will come flying out of the winter sun to save me. But I'm going to face this without begging, without crying. I can do that, at least. And I won't say I'm sorry, either. When you grow up like I did, you armor yourself however you can.

So that's it, I suppose. Sweet goddess, I can see the sun coming up, splashing off the snow, melting the ice off the bars. If I'm lucky, I have a little time left—an hour, maybe two. Time to sit here by myself and imagine what it might have been like: no more hunger, no lice, no backstabbing. Facing the world in silk and steel instead of rags. Maybe even a crowd chanting my name as I lead some foolhardy charge. *My* name, even though it's as common as weeds and bones. Chanting it like it was really part of this world, like it meant something.

BOOKS BY MICHAEL

FANTASY (RED ADEPT PUBLISHING)

The Dragonkin Trilogy

Wytchfire
Knightswrath
Kingsteel

The Godsfall Trilogy

The Dragonward
The Wintersea
The Undergod

Poetry

Leaving Iowa (Briery Creek Press)
Blue Collar Eulogies (Steel Toe Books)
Damnatio Memoriae (Brick Road Press)
What To Do If You're Buried Alive (Split Lip Press)
Ragged Eden (Glass Lyre Press)

ABOUT MICHAEL

Michael Meyerhofer is a fantasy author and poet living in Fresno, California. He is the author of two fantasy series, the Dragonkin Trilogy and the Godsfall Trilogy. He has also published five books of poetry. His work has appeared in *Asimov's Science Fiction Magazine, Orson Scott Card's InterGalactic Medicine Show, Rattle, Necessary Fiction, DIAGRAM,* and other journals. He has been the recipient of a number of awards, including the Whirling Prize, the James Wright Poetry Award, and the Laureate Prize. For more information and an embarrassing childhood photo, please visit wytchfire.com (fantasy) or troublewithhammers.com (poetry).

GET IN TOUCH

www.facebook.com/MeyerhoferTheAuthor
twitter.com/mrmeyerhofer
www.wytchfire.com
www.troublewithhammers.com
www.instagram.com/mrmeyerhofer

A Merry Mugging

A Christmas Short Story
(featuring Chris Barry of the Vigilante Series)

BY CLAUDE BOUCHARD

Tuesday, December 18, 2018
Montreal, 10:17 p.m.

Anxiety, fear and frustration summed up Mario Dupont's current state of mind – anxiety because of what he was planning to do, fear of what would actually happen when he tried and frustration stemming from the lack of opportunity to try so far.

There had been more people out and about earlier, not crowds but enough to be considered too many which increased the risk of potential problems. Then, as if someone had flicked a switch somewhere, the area had become deserted with only the occasional car on Notre-Dame and Charlevoix streets and no pedestrian traffic close by. These were, he reasoned, almost the ideal conditions, except he needed one person to walk by – just one.

His heart skipped a beat as a couple turned the corner and headed in his direction. He would have preferred dealing with only one person but these two, likely man and wife in their fifties, should be easy enough to handle once their fear set in. In addition, they just *looked* like folks with money so this might turn out to be more profitable than expected.

He pretended to be on his phone as they got closer, intent on not attracting their attention. For their part, they were having their own conversation and seemed oblivious of his presence. This would work out just fine.

"Well, all I can say is you certainly know how to impress a lady, Mr. Barry," said Sandy, hugging her husband's arm. "I've never been treated to a private concert before."

"We both have Martin to thank for that," Chris replied. "When he invited us over, I was expecting a few songs for sound checks, certainly not a full rehearsal of their show."

Sandy laughed. "As if they needed the practice. They're flawless."

"They're perfectionists – What the hell?" Chis exclaimed as they were suddenly shoved into the narrow alley they were passing.

"Just give me your wallets and I won't hurt you."

They turned toward their assailant, the young man they had just walked by on the street, who now blocked the way out, a knife in hand.

"You don't want to do this, buddy," said Chris. "Just leave us alone and we'll pretend it never happened."

"I-I'm serious," the young man insisted, not having expected any resistance.

Chris sighed then said, "Fine, but I don't like this," before reaching into his coat.

"Wait, what are you doing?" the man demanded, clearly nervous.

Chris stopped with his hand inside his coat and replied, "I'm getting my wallet. Isn't that what you wanted?"

"Well, yeah," said the man. "Just don't try anything stupid."

"Got it," said Chris before pulling out his Glock 26 – a favoured weapon for the millionaire turned clandestine government agent – and pointing it at their assailant's face. "Is this stupid?"

"Holy crap," the man exclaimed, instinctively dropping his blade and raising his hands above his head.

"Lean against the wall," Chris ordered.

"Look, can I just go?" the man pleaded, near tears.

"Against the wall," Chris repeated.

"I'm sorry," the man whimpered as he leaned against the wall. "I never should have tried doing this."

"Stop whining," said Chris while holstering his pistol. "I'm going to pat you down. If you move, I'll hurt you."

He frisked the young man and found no other weapons but relieved him of his wallet and mobile which he pocketed along with the switchblade Sandy had picked up in the interim.

"Okay, you're coming with us," said Chris.

"Am I under arrest?" asked the man, assuming Chris was a cop, not an agent with an elite secret agency.

"Not so far," Chris replied, "But that can change at any time. Let's go."

"Where are we going?" asked the man.

"The Italian place on the corner to sit down and chat," Chris replied. "It's freezing out here. If you decide to run, just remember I have your wallet and phone."

"Here we go," said the waiter. "Three Espressos and three Tiramisu."

"Thanks," said Chris before raising his cup to the young man boxed in the booth next to him. "To new acquaintances."

Embarrassed and surprised, the man glanced at Chris then at Sandy across from him before picking up his cup.

"Uh, cheers," he mumbled, staring at the table.

"What's your name?" Sandy asked.

"He has my wallet," the man sullenly replied. "He can check it out."

"Don't be an asshole," said Sandy.

The man blushed. "Mario, Mario Dupont."

"Thank you," said Sandy.

"This is weird," Mario muttered.

"What's weird?" asked Chris.

"Well, uh, I tried to mug you," Mario replied, "And now we're having coffee and cake. I don't have any money, by the way."

"Our treat," said Chris. "As for the weird part, isn't this better than if I'd shot you in the alley?"

"Well, yeah," Mario agreed, "But still."

Chris shrugged. "I felt like a snack while we chatted. So, how long have you been doing this mugging gig?"

Mario stared at the table again. "You probably won't believe me but this was my first time."

"I *do* believe you," said Chris. "You looked like you were crapping yourself. Why'd you do it?"

Mario blew out a breath and said, "I needed the money."

"What for?" asked Sandy, her tone soft. "Drugs? Debts?"

Mario squeezed his eyes shut tight as he shook his head. "I'm just broke. I lost my job a few months ago and I can't find another one, mostly because I haven't finished high school yet. I'm almost done now but so far, that's not good enough."

"I'm sorry to hear that," said Chris, "But you can't revert to robbing people on the street. You'll end up hurting someone, getting hurt or going to jail."

"I know," cried Mario as the tears began. "It was stupid but I'm desperate. If it was just me, I'd be okay but there's Katy and it's Christmas next week. I'm sorry."

"Who's Katy?" asked Sandy.

Mario wiped his eyes with a napkin, taking a moment to regain his composure before turning to Chris. "Can I have my phone for a minute? I want to show you something."

Chris fished the phone out of his coat pocket and handed it over. Mario tapped and scrolled then held it out to Sandy.

"That's my Katy," he said, his voice filled with pride.

"Aw, she's adorable," Sandy exclaimed, gazing at the photo of a curly blonde girl. "How old is she?"

"She just turned three," Mario replied and sighed. "She's such a good kid and deserves a better life than what she's getting."

"She should be reason enough for you to stay out of trouble," said Chris after Sandy passed him the phone.

"You're right," Mario admitted. "And I really mean it."

"Where is she now?" asked Sandy.

"My mom minds her when I'm not there," Mario replied. He hesitated then added, "With all the help she's given me, especially since Katy's mother disappeared, she's another reason why I shouldn't act stupid."

"Katy's mother disappeared?" Chris repeated.

"She left us," said Mario. "Turns out having a child wasn't as fun as she thought it would be and it cut into her party time too much."

"That's so sad," said Sandy.

"I'm glad she left," said Mario. "We're better off without her."

"How long ago did she leave?" asked Chris.

"Two years now," Mario replied. "Just before Katy's first birthday. I haven't heard from her since, which is how I want it. I'm proud to be bringing up my daughter by myself. She's a smart, funny, happy kid and we're doing fine together. I just wish I could find a job and get back to normal."

"What kind of work are you looking for?" asked Chris.

"Anything that would give me a regular paycheque," said Mario. "I was working in a warehouse for almost two years and liked it. I like physical work, it helps keep me in shape. Also, I can drive different kinds of forklifts and had no problem learning the inventory systems on the computer. My boss was sorry to let me go but cuts were made by seniority."

"You seem like a smart guy," said Chris.

Mario nodded and said, "I am, most of the time."

Chris gazed and him for a moment then said, "This little episode tonight, last time you'll ever pull something like that?"

"I swear," Mario vowed. "I'm sorry I even tried." He paused then added, "At least I was lucky to land on you two."

"Indeed," Chris agreed as he retrieved Mario's wallet from his coat and set it on the table. "Show me your driver's permit."

Mario pulled out his permit and slid it before Chris.

"Mind if I take a pic of that?" asked Chris.

"Uh, I guess not," Mario replied. "Why?"

"Because I want to check you out," said Chris, snapping a photo. "I'm pretty well connected so, as long as you don't turn out to be a lousy little shit, you should have a job to go to after the holidays."

"Are you serious?" Mario exclaimed.

"I wouldn't joke about something this important," Chris replied, pulling out a card on which all was printed was his name and a phone number. "Here's where you can reach me. What's your number?"

Dazed, Mario recited his mobile number which Chris recorded on his own phone.

"We're all set," said Chris once done. "Do you want anything else to eat?"

"No, thank you," Mario replied. "You've done more than enough as it is."

"Suit yourself," said Chris, pulling out his wallet. He put two twenties on the table to cover their order and tip then counted out another two hundred dollars which he held out to Mario.

"Oh, no," said Mario, shaking his head. "I can't take that."

Chris dropped the cash on the table and said, "Sure you can. It's for Katy."

"I don't believe this," Mario murmured as his eyes once again filled with tears. "What happened tonight?"

Chris smiled as he and Sandy slid out of the booth and replied, "A Merry Mugging."

BOOKS BY CLAUDE

THE VIGILANTE SERIES

Vigilante

The Consultant

Mind Games

The Homeless Killer

6 Hours 42 Minutes

Discreet Activities

Femme Fatale

Thirteen to None

The First Sixteen – The Prequel

See You in Saigon

Sins in the Sun

Getting Even

Make it Happen

The Nephew

Nasty in Nice

OTHER

ASYLUM
Something's Cooking

ABOUT CLAUDE BOUCHARD

Claude Bouchard was born in Montreal, Canada, at a very young age, where he still resides with his spouse, Joanne, under the watchful eye of Krystalle and Midnight, two black females of the feline persuasion. In a former life, he completed his studies at McGill University and worked in various management capacities for a handful of firms over countless years. From there, considering his extensive background in human resources and finance, it was a logical leap in his career path to stay home and write crime thrillers.

His first stab at writing fiction was actually in 1995, the result being his first novel, *Vigilante*. Two others of the same series followed by 1997 but all three remained dormant until publication in 2009. Since, besides writing *ASYLUM*, a standalone, the *Vigilante Series* has grown to fifteen thrilling installments including a revised version of *Nasty in Nice*, previously published on the now defunct Kindle Worlds platform.

Two of his novels were included in the pair of blockbuster *9 Killer Thriller* anthologies, the second of which made the USA Today Bestsellers list in March 2014. Claude has also penned *Something's Cooking*, a faux-erotica parody and cookbook under the pseudonyms Réal E. Hotte and Dasha Sugah. His books have topped the chart in the Vigilante Justice category on Amazon and over 600,000 copies have been distributed to date.

Claude's other interests include reading, playing guitar, painting, cooking, traveling and trying to stay in reasonable shape.

GET IN TOUCH:

Website: http://www.claudebouchardbooks.com
Twitter: https://twitter.com/ceebee308
Facebook: https://www.facebook.com/claude.bouchard2
Facebook (author page): https://www.facebook.com/ClaudeVigilanteBouchard
Amazon (author page): http://www.amazon.com/Claude-Bouchard/e/
B002BLL3RK

A Vanderbilt Christmas

BY NICOLE EVELINA

Victoria Woodhull was the first American woman to run for president of the United States in 1872. She was also a suffragist, spiritualist, and one of the first women to run a stock brokerage on Wall Street, along with her sister, Tennie. This is a fictionalized account of how Victoria may have become involved in the suffrage movement. The characters, their personalities, and the historical references are all accurate.

December 1868

If anyone had told me a year ago that I would be spending Christmas Eve at the home of Cornelius Vanderbilt, one of the richest men in the country, I would have booked them a room at Blackwell's Island with the other lunatics. Me? The guttersnipe daughter of a confidence man and a religious zealot whose favorite hobby was blackmailing people? Even with my gift of clairvoyance, it would have been too much to believe.

But then again, much had changed over the last year. When my sister Tennie and I moved to New York at the direction of my spirit guide, Demosthenes, we had no idea the good fortune that awaited us. Our Pa, no doubt sensing a way to make a quick buck, had arranged an introduction to Commodore Vanderbilt in the hopes he would employ us as mediums and magnetic healers. But the tycoon did him one better. After I successfully channeled the spirit of his long-dead mother and gave an accurate prediction of the stock market, he took us in as his assistants. Although, this may have had more to do with my sister's beauty than our skill.

No matter. We were here now. An invitation to Christmas Eve dinner was a rare honor, one much coveted by New York society. Ma and Pa would be fit-to-be-tied when they found out we were invited but they were not; but I thanked God their troublesome selves were back in the slums of Five Points where they belonged.

My husband, James, Tennie, and I, on the other hand, were seated along one side of a massive dining table that could easily seat twenty and was laden with china, crystal, and silver. The other chairs were occupied by a handful of the Commodore's close friends and business associates – including his rival Mr. Fisk – plus several generations of his family. Around us, wreaths of evergreen and holly decorated the damask covered walls and pine boughs dripped from an elegant gold chandelier, while wreaths of orange, bay, and cinnamon perfumed the air.

Across the table, the eldest Vanderbilt son, William, shot daggers at me and Tennie. Clearly his disposition toward us hadn't warmed any with time, nor had he grown in trust of us.

"Tell me, what will be your parlor trick tonight?" He picked at one of the starched white lace napkins. "Will you channel the angel who announced Christ's birth to the shepherds, or perhaps even the baby Jesus himself?"

"If you are so certain you know, perhaps you should place a bet on it," I shot back, referencing William's secret vice of gambling.

Before William could reply, a bevy of maids and footmen emerged from the kitchen carrying the first course of raw oysters. A succession of dishes followed, each more sumptuous than the last – broth, fried smelts, sweetbreads, turkey with cranberry sauce. We tucked in with enthusiasm and by the time the quail with truffles was served, any lingering awkwardness had vanished and even William was smiling, entertained by my husband's stories of his service in the Civil War.

Tennie and I were seated on either side of Mr. Vanderbilt, regaling him with stories of our clients. "What's the news south of Broadway?" he asked.

It was a polite way to inquire about the latest gossip from the brothels, where we still worked part-time as healers and many of New York's wealthiest businessmen took their pleasure. As a result, the Bowery's whores had more inside knowledge of business and government than the politicians in Washington.

I lowered my voice so that no one else would hear what I was about to say. "The spirits have a Christmas gift for you, Commodore." We had a tacit understanding that he wanted no knowledge of where I got the information for my stock tips; he preferred to let others believe they came from supernatural sources.

He leaned down as though to hear me better. "Oh, and what is that?"

"I am advised that stocks of Central Pacific Railroad are going to go up."

"Is that so? Well, I will see what I can do with that information. It has the potential to be very profitable for us both," he said, with a finger to the side of his nose, reminding me to keep the tip quiet.

I opened my mouth to say more but was distracted by Mr. Fisk calling to my husband from two seats away. "Say, James. You're a supporter of women's suffrage, are you not? What do you think of this split in the movement?" Only months before, the national women's suffrage organization had broken into two rival factions, each with a different philosophy about how best to achieve their goal.

Mr. Vanderbilt loudly harrumphed, "A well-deserved nail in their coffin, I say."

"Hey!" Tennie yelled. "How can you be so supportive of Vickie and me as independent businesswomen, but not want us to be able to vote? Isn't that our right as Americans?"

Mr. Vanderbilt squirmed in his seat. "Now, Tennie, don't get your dander up. I was just saying that those loudmouthed women can't lead our country to anything good." He patted her hand. "There's a might bit of difference between supporting your foray into finance and changing the law of the land." Elbowing his son, he added, "What's next? A woman president?" He guffawed.

William acknowledged his father with a forced smile, but his attention was on my husband, his expression far less fond than it had been just a minute before. "You support those sour spinsters?"

"Indeed, I do. I see no valid reason why women should not be granted the right to vote, especially seeing that former slaves can now do so." He turned to Mr. Fisk. "To answer your question, I believe the split is dangerous. Anyone who has ever been in the military knows that dissention among the ranks is a sign of weakness. A split is essentially mutiny against the current leaders." He shook his head. "It will be a hard climb back for them if they want to regain their momentum as a unified national movement."

"I don't know that it is so bad," I countered, sipping my wine. Most women would not dare contradict their husbands in public, but James was not an average man. He indulged me in most things, but especially whenever I showed interest in the woman's movement, which was beginning to appeal to me more and more.

"How so?"

"Well, from what I've read in the papers, it seems to me Mrs. Stone and her ilk are content to let things play out as they will, whereas Miss Anthony and Mrs.

Stanton are much more willing to take risks. If life has taught me anything, it's that if women want to get ahead, we must do whatever needs done."

"Watch out, James," Mr. Vanderbilt, said conspiratorially. "Your Victoria could well become one of them, from the sounds of things."

"I do hope so! In fact –"

His thought was interrupted by the butler, who silently slipped into the room to whisper into Mr. Vanderbilt's ear. But before the Commodore could reply, my name drifted in from several rooms away, called by a male voice.

Pa. And where he was, Ma was sure to follow. What were they doing here?

Around the table, heads turned and conversation ceased as guests sought the source of the interruption.

I looked down at my lap, mortified, ears and cheeks burning. All I had wanted was one night – just one – of peace when I could forget the calamity and embarrassment that was my family and the poverty of my upbringing. I was going places, poised to join the blue-bloods who ran this town and tonight was supposed to be my unofficial introduction to that world. Now that opportunity was ruined.

Mr. Vanderbilt gestured to the table and replied in a tone too quiet for me to hear. But William must have understood because he leapt to his feet. He was almost at the French doors when they flew open, admitting the astringent scent of gin moments before Ma came into view, calling, "Happy Christmas!" Her garish red and green tartan gown overpowered her small, boney frame, making her look like someone had mistaken her for a gift to be placed under the tree.

She wobbled a bit and Tennie stood to steady her. "You aren't drunk, are you, Ma? Please don't tell me you are."

"Nah," she brayed. "Just had a nip." She lifted a small bottle from her reticule and wiggled it.

I grabbed the bottle when Ma made to brandish again. "Best keep that hidden for now."

Following behind, Pa handed William his coat and hat as though he was a servant and sidled up to Mr. Vanderbilt. He extended his hand to shake. "Sorry we're late, but our invitation must 'ave gotten lost in the mail."

Mr. Vanderbilt took in Pa's tattered waistcoat and faded breeches and hesitantly accepted his hand. "I – ah, yes…"

Pa barreled over his attempted response. "Cuz, you're too gracious a' gent to overlook the man who brought these find lasses to your door, am I right?" Pa winked at Tennie and me. "When I heard down at the pub that my girls had snagged an invitation, I said to my Anne, 'there's got to be some mistake.' So here we are." He pulled out an empty chair and plopped down as though he really had been invited.

Around us, mouths hung open and eyes were wide with shock.

There was no way Tennie and I would get out of this with our reputations intact, but I had to try. Putting my arm around Ma and nudging her toward the door, I said, "It seems you have missed both dinner and dessert. Perhaps it would be best if you called another time so you can enjoy a proper meal with the Vanderbilts."

Following my lead, William held out Pa's coat and hat. "Yes, that would be splendid. Shall we say some time in the new year?" His tone made it clear their invitation was for the tenth of never, but neither one seemed to notice.

"Nonsense," the Commodore boomed. "Let them stay. They are Victoria and Tennie's family and if there is one thing Christmas is about, it's family."

Instead of the men retiring to one room for cigars and port and the women to another for gossip and brandy or tea, as was traditionally done, Mr. Vanderbilt invited us all into his parlor for a game of Whist, one of his favorite pastimes. Several of the guests, Mr. Fisk included, begged off to return home to their families, but I suspected they really wanted to be away from my parents and gossip about the unexpected turn the night had taken.

The parlor was decorated similarly to the dining room, with pine garland looped around banisters and hanging from the mantle of the black marble fireplace. Miniature candles in tiny sconces on the tree and flickering candles in crystal chandeliers gave the room a festive glow, which was enhanced by the Christmas carols Mr. Vanderbilt's eldest daughter played on the piano, while her sister sang.

James and I arranged ourselves around a small rectangular wooden table, opposite Mr. Vanderbilt and Tennie, while at another, William and his wife reluctantly took up their places as my parents' competitors. As we played, two maids ensured our cups stayed full of warm spiced rum punch and the men's cigars remained lit.

Tennie and I won our first two games but lost the third and by the time James laid down his final card in the fourth game, my cheeks were glowing with merriment. Perhaps tonight would turn out well after all.

But then a chair crashed to the ground behind us as William shot to his feet. "She cheated." He pointed at my mother. "You cheated. How dare you –"

Ma stood as well, hands on her hips, facing William down. "I did no such thing." She leaned over the table and poked a finger in William's chest. "You take that back."

William turned to his wife. "Did you see the way she dealt that hand? Overhand shuffle is a sure sign of a card shark."

"If anyone would know, it's him," Tennie whispered to me.

"Ladies, gentlemen, please. This is only a friendly holiday game," the Commodore reminded everyone, while attempting to draw his son away from the table. "I'm happy to repay any wagers lost. I'll see no one returns home tonight poorer than when they arrived."

But Pa would not be so easily dissuaded. "Fine thing, calling my wife a liar and a cheat on Christmas. I thought you toplofty gents were supposed to have manners."

William's eyes widened. "What did you call me, sir?"

"You 'eard me. I don't 'preciate you being all high-toned with us and assuming we cheat 'cause we 'ave to earn our coin while you were born into yours."

The two exchanged a few more heated words while Tennie and I helped Ma, who was crying now, over to the chaise lounge against one wall. Tennie sat next to her, cooing calming words into her ear and petting her like a child. "We'll be fine here," she assured me. "Go take care of Pa. Their bluster should burn out soon."

Or not. I turned in time to see William's fist connect with Pa's jaw.

Pa grunted and instinctively pushed William back, knocking him into the Christmas tree, which wavered, then toppled to the floor. Several of the candles affixed to its branches came loose and bounced onto the Turkish rug, which was quickly set ablaze.

Tennie screamed, followed by one of Mr. Vanderbilt's daughters. Thick black smoke dimmed the room and I rushed toward the windows, yanking them open as fast as I could. James threw a blanket on the fire to smother it at the same time as Mr. Vanderbilt dumped a bucket of sand on it. Together, they were able to douse the flames and extinguish the remaining candles before the fire spread or did any serious damage. Carefully, they raised the tree so that it once again stood tall.

"Damn thing. I feared this would happen," Mr. Vanderbilt groused.

"I am so sorry," I apologized on behalf of my parents, who made no move to do so. "Please take the cost of the rug out of my paycheck."

Mr. Vanderbilt looked up at me, his eyes kind. "Nonsense. These things happen." He gestured to the bucket of sand. "Why do you think we had this on hand? Damn candles are a hazard."

Turning to his son, he growled, "William, we will discuss your behavior later. Now, I think it is best if you cool your heels." He gestured toward the door.

Grumbling, William stormed out.

Mr. Vanderbilt bowed to my parents. "I do apologize for my son's unacceptable behavior. Please, let me make it up to you." He gestured toward the floor, where a pile of finely-wrapped presents peeked out from the soot and sand. "Please take one. It is the least I can do."

Ma's face lit up at the prospect of a fancy gift. "Thank ya kindly." She pawed through the sand, weighing packages and inspecting her options, no doubt looking for the most valuable gift. If anyone could sniff it out, it would be her.

Meanwhile, Pa spoke with Mr. Vanderbilt in hushed tones. "You know, if you have a mind to set things right, I have a supply of elixir in my shop that would benefit you and your friends. Perhaps you could give me an in? My tonics cure most ills, from bum knees to gout and even kidney ailments. I hear tell you have a spot of rheumatism…"

I rolled my eyes. Pa's formulas were little more than alcohol and beef fat, with a few herbs thrown in for good measure. I turned to warn Tennie that Pa was trying to swindle her sweetheart, and caught Ma slipping a small, thin package from beneath the tree into her purse. This wouldn't be a problem, had she not already accepted one package, which Pa held under his arm.

Before I could say anything, much less rescue the purloined present, Mr. Vanderbilt was ushering them toward the door with more apologies and wishes for a joyous holiday season. Ma grinned a secret smile at me as they departed, silently gloating over having put one over on the tycoon.

"What a night," I sighed deeply once we were home safely and sprawled in the comfort of our own modest parlor.

"Well, at least Ma didn't tell any embarrassing stories," Tennie said.

"I think nearly burning down the house of the wealthiest man in New York is gift enough," I said dryly. "Word is sure to get out. I'm sure no one will include us on their guest lists now."

"I wouldn't be too sure." James rummaged in his coat pocket. "I was just about to give you this when your family intervened." He handed me a small envelope. "Open it."

I slid a gloved finger beneath the flap and removed a square sheet of paper, scanning it quickly.

National Convention of Woman Suffrage
Annual Convention
Washington D.C.
January 19-20

Admit One

I looked up at him in wonder. "What is this?"

A sparkling smile lit his face. "Your ticket into suffrage high society. Demosthenes told you that you would one day hold a position of great authority in this country. I aim to make that come true. This is the perfect place to begin. Besides, this way you can evaluate Miss Anthony and Mrs. Stanton for yourself before you decide which faction to join. No one will give a hoot what your parents did once you've made yourself known to this group."

Was it possible? Could James be correct? Perhaps this really was the beginning of a new era for me, one even my family couldn't ruin. That would be a Christmas miracle indeed.

I threw my arms around him. "Thank you so much. Your support means the world to me."

"Happy Christmas, Victoria."

"Happy Christmas, James."

The End

BOOKS BY NICOLE

Madame Presidentess (biographical historical fiction about Victoria Woodhull)

Daughter of Destiny (Guinevere's Tale Book 1) (Arthurian historical fantasy)

Camelot's Queen (Guinevere's Tale Book 2) (Arthurian historical fantasy)

Mistress of Legend (Guinevere's Tale Book 3) (Arthurian historical fantasy)

The Guinevere's Tale Trilogy (compendium of the three books above)

Been Searching for You (contemporary romance/women's fiction)

The Once and Future Queen: Guinevere in Arthurian Legend (non-fiction)

ABOUT NICOLE

Nicole Evelina is a historical fiction, non-fiction, and women's fiction author whose six books have won more than 30 awards, including three Book of the Year designations. Her fiction tells the stories of strong women from history and today, with a focus on biographical historical fiction, while her non-fiction focuses on women's history, especially sharing the stories of unknown or little-known figures.

Nicole's writing has appeared in *The Huffington Post, The Philadelphia Inquirer, The Independent Journal, Curve Magazine* and numerous historical publications. She is one of only six authors who completed a week-long writing intensive taught by #1 *New York Times* bestselling author Deborah Harkness.

Nicole is currently working on her next historical fiction novel, which centers on an obscure WWII heroine, and researching two future non-fiction books. You can find her online at http://nicoleevelina.com/.

GET IN TOUCH

https://twitter.com/NicoleEvelina
http://www.goodreads.com/nicoleevelina
http://pinterest.com/nicoleevelina/
https://www.facebook.com/nicolccvelinapage/
http://instagram.com/nicoleevelina
http://nicoleevelina.com

Another Bloody Festival

BY CIARA BALLINTYNE

Alloran's boots beat out a rapid tattoo as he strode down the hallway. It was the eve of a momentous moment, and no one else even realised it.

He hurried through the hallways towards his laboratory, running through the last calculations in his head. It was vitally important to be sure the math was correct, the rune-chains linked properly, and the spellwork perfect to the finest detail. Even the most infinitesimal of errors could spell total—

"Well, excuse me!"

He blinked down at the sorceress he'd just bumped into. Ismyn—yellow-eyed, red-haired, her creamy skin gorgeous against the gold and black brocade she wore.

"Oh, Alloran!" Her expression of affront melted away, replaced by a coy smile as she reached out and twined a lock of his unkempt and overlong black hair around one finger. "Why—are *you* coming to the winter solstice feast? I didn't think anything could drag you out of your laboratory!"

For the first time, the sounds of merry-making permeated the haze of calculations engulfing his mind. He was standing right at the entrance to one of the citadel's great halls. The double doors stood open, revealing a room full of long tables. Various wizards and sorceresses were arriving to take their seats, and musicians played harps in one corner of the room, the waterfall of sound almost lost beneath the hubbub of chatter. Great glittering streamers of magic in red and gold and green decorated the room's ceiling. Vases of roses, encircled with holly wreaths, marched down the centre of each table, and the flickering candlelight gave the room an old-world feel compared to the usual steady burn of wizard glows.

Another bloody festival.

"Uh…no," he said. "I have important work waiting for me."

He circled around her, and she muttered something as he walked away. He glanced back at her, almost walking into a wall as he tried to cut the corner. Had that been "Such a waste"?

He shook his head and hurried on, returning to his calculations. When he reached his laboratory, he paused with the door half-open to check the wards woven through the walls. It was absolutely imperative that everything was contained within these walls tonight. Satisfied, he strode into his laboratory. Dozens of wizard glows hung from the ceiling, and he blinked in their brilliance.

"Someone give me an update!"

The room was large and contained numerous workbenches, including one that ran around the entire outside wall. One of the central benches held a spindly construction of thin timber rods and gold wire. The half-dozen assistants in the room were engaged in a flurry of activity everywhere other than around this construct; they were packing various items from the benches into boxes and winding up rolls of wire while yelling across the room at each other.

"T minus 10 minutes, sir!" shouted Kevaughn. His first assistant was a scrawny looking young man in utilitarian shirt and pants that were too large for him. He had his sleeves rolled up and a haystack of black hair on his head.

Alloran snagged another assistant, this one a young woman in spectacles, who was clearing a bench of clutter. "Make sure you take that." He indicated what looked like an innocuous jewellery box. "The spells on that aren't anything we want in the vicinity of the gate."

The girl started—*what was her name again?*—then stuffed the box in with a sword and what looked like a half-completed lantern. He was proud of that one—a wizard glow in a box, he called it. An unending source of illumination for the common man, once it was done. Well, one man, anyway. Someone else could mass-produce them, if they wished. Once he'd solved the puzzle and made the thing work, he'd be bored with it.

The girl hurried from the room with her box, others filing after her. They had a secondary location to take all his magical projects—things that were incomplete and thus sensitive and items that carried volatile spells—which couldn't be risked near *this* particular magical working when it was brought to fruition. And *this* was why he told wizards never to keep half-completed teleport spells in their rooms. Maybe they would listen when one of them finally blew themselves up.

His gaze swept the lab, checking that everything that should go had gone. He grabbed the last straggler by his coat, a boy with indigo eyes the same shade as his own, and nodded at a brass kettle resting on the bench. "That one, too."

The boy scurried out, the kettle swinging from his arm, and Alloran gave a satisfied nod. It was just him, Kevaughn, and the gate now.

"The spells are in order?" he asked, sweeping through the ranks of benches to join Kevaughn.

"Of course, sir. Just as you left them." The young man grinned up at him toothily, obviously pleased to be involved in what he considered to be the greatest magical feat of the century with the most renowned research wizard alive. Which, of course, it was, and so he should. Alloran's best friend, Ladanyon, would be bilious with jealousy if the gate worked.

Alloran brushed past to do a final inspection of the construct. It was a gate to a hell. He wasn't sure *which* circle of hell, only that it would be one of them. Ancient wizards had peeked through the veil, so he should be able to identify the hell by its features and denizens, but a gate, through which a man might pass… Well, his head anyway. He hadn't made this one large enough to walk through. He wouldn't visit on this first attempt, only check it worked. Then he could think about practical applications, such as siphoning dimensional energies to create new power sources….

He shook his head, realising he was distracting himself with the limitless possibilities, and adopted a stance before the gate. He checked the spell sequences already in place, making sure they were correct and intact, then laid the final rune set, sketching them into the air in indigo fire with one hand.

The runes flashed bright, then faded away as they ignited the spell sequences. There was a flash of light in the centre of the framework, in the middle of the 'door' shape, but it was there and gone so fast; it was almost the deception of an eye blink.

"Did it work?" Kevaughn asked uncertainly.

Alloran licked his lips and then boldly thrust his arm into the construct, half-expecting—though he would never confess it—to see his hand emerge out the other side.

It didn't.

Kevaughn gasped, then whooped in excitement. Alloran pulled his hand out, flexing his fingers, checking that everything still functioned as it should. It did; of course it did—this gate, this *hell* gate, was based on the same principles of portal magic, long tried and tested spells with no side effects.

Alloran shoved his head through the portal, gasping again as new vistas opened up before him—and from the shock of the cold. It was freezing in this hell, so cold that his cheeks stiffened with it, and his teeth began to chatter. There was nothing to see except endless tundra, the snow and ice swept smooth and hard by the katabatic winds wailing across it.

He jerked back into the almost-painful warmth of his lab, turning to Kevaughn with an excited if frozen grin forced into the cold-stiffened muscles of his face. "It worked! It's the seventh hell."

"Can I see?" Kevaughn's face shone with excitement. "Please, sir?"

Alloran nodded his permission, stepping away and folding his arms to watch the young wizard receive his reward.

Kevaughn leaned into the gate, preparing to enter a new dimension.

Something gangling and black leapt out of the gate. Kevaughn screamed. Blood, shockingly red, splashed across the walls and floor. Kevaughn crumpled, giving Alloran a brief look at his ruined face and gashed throat. Alloran backed up, bile rising in his throat, until he bumped into a bench. Seven hells, Kevaughn... he was... dead.

The demon—a seventh-hell imp—had landed lightly on the opposite bench, and now it cast around, its face lifted as if scenting the air. It was a little larger than a monkey, barely small enough to fit through the gate, but with elongated limbs that made it look spider-like as it crouched. It had a flat face set with dull, red eyes, and long pointed ears swept back from its skull. It was black and hairless. Vicious claws curved from the end of each digit on its six-fingered hands, and fangs protruded from an almost lipless mouth.

The imp turned its face to Alloran. He stared at it, paralysed by shock, his mind fumbling for something—anything—that he could do, *should* do, but the spells kept slipping from his mind, like elusive fish sliding from grasping fingers.

Then the imp threw itself across the room, bounding from bench to bench, to cast itself directly at the door. Alloran took a half-step forward, one hand lifted—and then the imp sailed straight through the solid door and all the wards cast into it.

Alloran gaped. Not only had the magic failed to stop it, but the imp could phase-shift! It had clearly been solid enough when it killed Kevaughn, but it had done something to allow it to pass directly through solid matter, shifting its own particles so they no longer aligned with those of the door.

Need to move, need to do something—before it kills anyone else.

Reluctantly, he forced himself to hurry to the door. His thoughts raced as he yanked it open. He would be sanctioned for this, no doubt. Would they take his research away?

He glanced back at the dead youth's corpse. Maybe they should.

As soon as the door opened, he heard the screams.

"Seven hells!" This time he managed to break into a run, following the sound of the terror. Sweat trickled down his back. What could he do to contain the thing? To kill it? For the first time in his life, creativity failed him.

He passed another body—an elderly sorceress sprawled in her own blood, her chest and stomach torn open—while another woman cowered against the wall. Seeing Alloran, she screamed, then sagged in relief.

"My magic, it just…just… did nothing!" she gibbered.

Alloran ran on. The imp had gone in the direction of the feast hall, likely drawn on by the sound of the merry-making. Ahead, the music erupted into a cacophony of wrong notes and then died.

More panicked wails began.

He accelerated, bursting through the hall doors into a nightmare of blood and fleeing people. It was impossible to know how many were down, but it seemed everyone still able was running. He managed to clear the door just before the closest stampeded out.

He scanned the hall, trying to find the imp. There it was, bounding from table to table, scattering plates of food and cutlery behind it in a raucous explosion of smashing crockery, slaying a person here and another there with casual swipes of its vicious hands. There was a strange kind of grin plastered to its thin-lipped face—manic delight.

The people at the door trying to escape were still bottlenecked, but as the room emptied, it became apparent that some were fighting back. A group of sword sorceresses and wizards, predominantly reds, were forming ranks. The front rank held large swords and halberds. They advanced on the imp, while the second and third ranks prepared spells.

With a shout, he lunged forward, directing an indigo blast of magic at the imp. It struck it and knocked it clear off the table in a clatter of silver against porcelain, but then the imp popped up onto the table again, apparently unhurt. Its grin widened, and it deliberately licked blood from its talons.

The platoon attacked. Coordinated blasts of magic struck the imp from one side. The energy, red shot through with strands of blue and orange, hit the imp again. This time it bounded away, expending the blast's force, and when it halted, faint tendrils of smoke rose from its skin.

Undeterred, the sword sorceresses and wizards systematically blasted the imp.

"It's not working!" Alloran cried, but they either didn't hear him over the noise of their own magic, or they didn't care. Frustrated, he swept a vase of flowers from a nearby table, ignoring the water that spilled across the tablecloth. What else could he do?

He blasted the imp again, this time shaping the energy so that it sliced rather than exploded. The imp yelped, evidently taken aback by the change in attack. The blade of sizzling blue energy cut open the imp's hide—but no blood came forth. The imp looked at its own injury, then at Alloran, and its grin widened again.

Then it charged straight at him.

Seven hells! He'd done something to get its attention. Had it identified him as a threat because he'd changed his approach? Alloran dodged away, skidding on loose cutlery as he went. Did that mean there *was* a way to kill the thing? His left foot went out from under him, betrayed by a fork, and he went down, catching hold of the tablecloth. It did nothing to support him, and instead pulled free in a tremendous crash of decorative candelabra and plates of meat. The candles doused with a hiss in the pools of water from the fallen vase.

The imp was coming straight at him, bounding into the air one more time in a leap that would land it on his face. Blasts of red magic struck it to no effect. Desperate, Alloran threw the tablecloth at the imp. It billowed out, tangling the imp in its folds. Then he remembered the thing could phase shift. He cowered, his arms over his head, waiting for the imp to sail free of the cloth.

It didn't. Instead, it writhed and howled. A green patch bloomed on the white cloth. Demon ichor… But from what? The cut he'd inflicted on the imp had achieved nothing—no blood had been shed.

He stood, backing away uncertainly to give the imp room. It was flailing, tearing the cloth from its body by shredding it with its claws. He could see its wildly grinning face and then its belly.

Green blood dripped from the wound where he'd sliced it with magic. But… why?

Something had changed. Something had made it vulnerable. The cloth? Surely not; it was simple linen, with no magical properties….

The water. The cloth had been sodden with water from the vase he'd knocked over. The imp was not only tearing the cloth away, but was shaking its various limbs, like a dog shedding water.

"Water!" he shouted. "Water makes it vulnerable to cutting. We need to douse it in water and then cut it apart!"

He raced to the next table and grabbed a vase of roses. He didn't even bother to pull the flowers free before hurling the whole thing at the imp.

The demon broke free of the cloth. Seeing the vase hurtling at it, it dodged—too wet to phase-shift?—but the glass struck the tiled floor and shattered, splashing water all over the demon. It howled and tried to shake itself free. But another quick-witted sword sorceress dashed forwards with another vase.

"Cut it!" Alloran shouted. "We have to cut it! The water only makes it vulnerable; it doesn't hurt it."

He demonstrated, attacking the imp with two whirling blades of indigo energy, slashing it in numerous places until the front rank of sword wizards and sorceresses closed with their weapons, blocking his access.

"It won't die!" someone cried.

"Hack it apart!" Alloran shouted.

He pushed his way into the crowd, now starting to stand down and shoulder swords and halberds, to see the bloody work. The imp had been reduced to pieces lying in a pool of green ichor, but they still squirmed. The detached head even blinked at him, and Alloran's stomach flopped over.

"It won't burn," a sorceress said, and she demonstrated. The flames licked over the twitching parts, then died.

"We can send it back through the gate," Alloran said.

"Your gate has already been dismantled," a cool voice said.

Alloran grimaced, both at the idea his construct had been destroyed and at the owner of the voice. He pivoted to face a hawk-profiled red wizard. "Valgon."

Valgon carried no weapon and wore no armour, but he radiated a deadliness no other sword wizard present could match. "As soon as I saw your involvement, I dispatched a squad to destroy any active items in your lab."

Alloran tried to keep his expression smooth, but from the grim look of satisfaction on Valgon's face, he failed. Valgon was the commander of the citadel guard, and well within his rights to act as he had. But he was angling for a place on the Council of Wizards, and Alloran had no doubt this was a political power grab. "Well then, I could open another gate—"

"You'll be lucky if you'll be allowed to continue researching," Valgon said coldly. "Much less open another gate."

A sick feeling grew in Alloran's stomach as he stared around at the carnage. Valgon was right. Easily twenty men and women had been slaughtered by the imp, plus Kevaughn. Why hadn't he thought of this? He'd had containment wards on the lab, but the imp had sailed right through them. Why had he given no consideration to the special characteristics of demons—such as imperviousness to magic?

He couldn't do this anymore. He had to stop. But…but he wouldn't. He *knew* he wouldn't. When he researched, nothing was off-limits, nothing so taboo that it could not be studied. The puzzle was more important. *Solving* the puzzle was all that mattered.

A lump grew in his throat, and he swallowed hard. The only way—to stop himself, to save lives—would be to stop altogether. Quit research magic. Walk away from the puzzle.

The very idea made his chest tighten to the point where he grew dizzy. No, it was the right thing to do. He'd stop. He *would*.

"Box up the pieces individually," Valgon was saying. "And then scatter them. I'm going to burn all the research."

Alloran's head jerked up. *Burn* his research? This had been a mistake, no doubt—he would be making no more hell gates. But to *burn* the knowledge was criminal. "You can't—"

He swallowed anything else he might have said as Valgon nailed him with a gimlet glare.

"Did you have something more you wished to say?" he asked, staring down his nose.

"No." Alloran shook his head. Maybe he could rescue some notes from his rooms while Valgon searched the lab. "No, nothing."

He watched mutely as Valgon rounded up enough sword wizards and sorceresses to get the job done and marched them from the room. When they were gone, he glanced around cautiously. There were a few people picking through the wreckage, but no one with any authority. He slid towards the door, watching to see if anyone noticed or—worse—tried to stop him.

No one did. He clenched his hands, chafing against the slow pace he was forcing himself to maintain to avoid drawing attention, his back prickling as he waited for a shout to call him back. When he reached the door, he stepped into the hallway to find Valgon still there. He shrank back.

"Take ten people and burn all the notes in the lab," Valgon said to a red wizard. "Stalyia, you do the same in Alloran's rooms. I'm going to ask the Lord Wizard for an arrest warrant."

Alloran swallowed a gasp. Arrest him! He'd broken no laws...but people had died. There needed to be an investigation, and he'd no doubt it would be a long one. By the time he was released, everything would be lost.

Reflexively, he started running through the math in his mind, but several lines in, he faltered. Had he gotten those two operations around the right way? He wasn't sure. It was just the stress, the pressure making him question himself...

But what if in several months, when they cleared him, he really *had* forgotten? It was pages and pages of mathematical formula and rune sequences...

He bolted. A few corridors away, he stopped, breathing hard and leaning on his knees. Now if he could find some parchment and ink, he could try and write down everything he remembered, and maybe he could hide it until he could come back and retrieve it. Somewhere it would be safe until all the kerfuffle died down.

Not because he meant to use it. No, he'd decided to stop, and that was that: no more research magic for him. No, this was just because knowledge should be preserved. It was just to save it, for its own sake.

It was...just in case.

BOOKS BY CIARA

THE SEVEN CIRCLES OF HELL

Confronting the Demon

Stalking the Demon

Becoming the Demon

Being the Demon (coming soon)

THE SUNDERED OATH

In the Company of the Dead

On the Edge of Death

To Make the Dead Weep

ABOUT CIARA

Ciara Ballintyne grew up on a steady diet of adult epic fantasy from the age of nine, leaving her with a rather confused outlook on life – she believes the good guys should always win, but knows they often don't. She is an oxymoron; an idealistic cynic.

She began her first attempts at the craft of writing in 1992, culminating in the publication of her debut work, *Confronting the Demon*, in 2013. Her first book to be published with Evolved Publishing is *In the Company of the Dead*.

She holds degrees in law and accounting, and is a practising financial services lawyer. In her spare time, she speculates about taking over the world – how hard can it really be? If she could be anything, she'd choose a dragon, but if she is honest she shares more in common with Dr. Gregory House of House M.D. – both the good and the bad. She is a browncoat, a saltgunner, a Whedonite, a Sherlockian, a Ringer and a Whovian… OK, most major geek fandoms. Her alignment is chaotic good. She is an INTJ.

Ciara lives in Sydney, Australia, with her husband, her two daughters, and a growing menagerie of animals that unfortunately includes no dragons.

GET IN TOUCH

Twitter: @CiaraBallintyne
Facebook: http://facebook.com/CiaraBallintyne
Website: http://ciaraballintyne.com
Email: ciaraballintyne@hotmail.com

Holiday in Hartland

BY GAIL CLEARE

B ridget Reilly tugged another piece of firewood off the stack on the back porch and added it to the pile already in her arms. She squinted her eyes up at the white sky, where large, lazy snowflakes drifted into focus and zigzagged down through the foggy air. One of them hit her smack on the forehead with an icy splash, and she pulled in her head like a turtle so the hood of her puffy ski jacket shielded her face.

She still wasn't used to the winters up here in Vermont. Until last year, she'd spent most of her holiday vacations sunbathing in the tropics. What did she know about shoveling snow, driving on black ice, or stockpiling firewood and batteries in case of a blizzard? Before she'd moved here, Bridget had lived in Virginia, where snow was an exotic rarity. Her ex-husband had hired people to take care of the garden, and the fireplace was fueled by gas.

She did most of the household chores herself now. Amazing, how people could change. Bridget got along fine without depending on help. The freedom to simply be herself, without struggling to impress anyone, was a massive relief after all those years of thinking she had to dress herself up as bait to catch some powerful man. That was over now, thank God. Three husbands and three divorces were more than enough failures for anyone to bear.

Bridget had turned the page in her life story. She'd left her high-end interior design business in the hands of her capable staff and gone away on an extended vacation, while husband number three worked out his anger issues. The lakeside cottage in the cozy little town of Hartland, Vermont, was the perfect hideaway. It had belonged to her mother, and no one in Bridget's old life knew it existed.

Living here alone after Mom's death had made Bridget more independent. Her sister, Nell, came to visit now and then, but this past year it had mostly been Bridget, her toy poodle Lulu, and Mom's dog Winston, a West Highland Terrier. Just the three of them, unless she felt like company. Friendly townspeople who had known and loved her mother invited Bridget to dinner parties and community events. She'd mastered the art of declining in a polite, but firm, way. Most of the time, she preferred being alone. Reinventing herself yet again was hard work, and Bridget had a lot to think about.

She turned her head and glanced into the woods, reassured to glimpse holiday lights glimmering through the trees. Yesterday, she'd helped Jake string them up on his porch. She'd insisted and wisely, he'd caved in. One of Mom's closest friends for much of her life and in love with her for most of that time, he knew exactly how stubborn the Reilly women could be.

Jake didn't intrude on Bridget's solitude, but he welcomed her whenever she called or appeared at his door. Their friendship was solid, based on helping one another through dark times and emerging safely from the other end of the tunnel. Bridget owed him a lot. If it weren't for Jake's encouragement, she would never have started looking for her daughter again.

She clambered up the stairs to the back porch, burdened by the heavy logs, and kicked her boots against the top step to knock off the snow. Then she flipped the storm door open with her foot and entered the kitchen. She balanced against a kitchen chair while she slid out of her wet boots and left them on the mat by the door. Balancing the firewood carefully, she went through to the living room and stacked it into the box near the hearth. Bridget pulled aside the fire screen and tossed another log on the fire, then poked the embers until it caught and slid the screen back into place.

Lulu and Winston watched from their matching beds, placed strategically near the fireplace. They wiggled their tails and smiled but didn't budge from their warm nests. Winston leaned his head over and licked Lulu's ear. She rolled onto her back and showed her belly, poking him with one petite paw. When Bridget made a kissy sound, they both turned to look at her, ears perked.

She laughed. "No, it's not time for dinner yet. Don't worry, I won't forget."

Glancing at the clock on the bookcase, she went back into the kitchen to hang her coat on a hook by the door. Stopping to stir the big pot of homemade chicken soup that bubbled on the stove, she tasted it and adjusted the seasoning.

A loaf of fresh-baked sourdough bread sat on the wooden cutting board, tempting her, but she pulled herself away and ran upstairs to brush her hair and refresh her lipstick. She looked into the guest room on her way past. Everything looked neat and comfortable, and the scent of the cinnamon candle she'd lit earlier hung in the air.

She'll be here soon. Oh my baby, my sweet girl.

The image of a small pink face flashed through her mind, with the memory of a baby's hoarse cry. Then the vision morphed into the pretty face she'd seen just two months prior, the adult woman that infant had become. Bridget had looked deep into Lizzie's eyes, and suddenly all those lost years felt insignificant. Her daughter had seemed nervous and emotional, but who wouldn't in that situation? Bridget hoped that by now, Lizzie'd been able to get used to the idea that the woman she'd always thought was her mother, was really her grandmother, and the man she'd thought was her older brother, was really her father.

Hoping the snow wasn't too bad on the highway, Bridget went back downstairs and settled into an armchair by the front windows. On the footstool in front of her was a photo album. She picked it up and thumbed through it again.

Here they are, her grandparents, great aunts, uncles, and cousins. Six generations of the Reilly clan, collected on these pages.

Mom had kept a stack of photo albums in the cupboard behind the television in the den. Bridget had spent the last week going through them, pulling a few prints here and there, to make up a sampler of the family history. On the last page, she'd put a print of the shot Nell had taken with her cell phone in October, and an orange maple leaf that Bridget had pressed and saved from that day. The photo showed the two of them, Bridget and her daughter, standing close together with their arms entwined. They had the same face, the Reilly blue eyes, and long blond hair. If it weren't for eighteen years between them, someone might take them for sisters. Nobody would ever have suspected the two had just met for the second time, the first being the day Lizzie was born and had disappeared from Bridget's life.

Wondering how the girl would react when she saw the pictures, Bridget put the album aside and gazed across the room at the spruce tree she'd set up in the corner. Decorated with garlands of popcorn and cranberries strung with a needle and thread, it was hung with pinecones and fresh-water mussel shells that she'd dipped in sparkly gold and silver paint and tied with red and green ribbons. At the very top was a star she'd made of twisted grapevine, painted gold. White fairy lights twinkled in the branches, and under the tree several prettily wrapped packages looked intriguing and mysterious.

After glancing at the clock again, she brought the album into the kitchen, where a roll of Christmas paper and ribbons waited.

It was late when she finally heard the sound of a car in the driveway. Curled up on the sofa with a book, Bridget raised her head to listen. A car door slammed, so she went to open the front door.

She'd left on the holiday lights that decorated the porch and the lamp post. Lizzie stood at the bottom of the front steps in the multi-colored glow, a suitcase beside her. Her face looked tired and drawn. Without a word, Bridget opened her arms wide and her daughter stepped into them. She buried her face in Bridget's shoulder and they stood together amid the swirling snowflakes, locked in a hug that had been a long time coming.

"Thank you," Lizzie said. "For being here. For letting me come."

"Are you kidding?" Bridget held her closer. "I've been waiting twenty-five years to celebrate Christmas with you!"

Her daughter looked up, smiling. "Merry Christmas, um…Bridget."

"Come inside? I've got hot soup, and two small furry people who want to meet you." Lulu and Winston stood just inside the door, dancing with excitement.

Lizzie got her bag and dragged it up the steps. "Sounds like heaven."

They went inside and closed the door.

"And this is my Aunt Katie, my mother's sister. She always had the most gorgeous clothes. Nell and I adored her."

Lizzie turned the page, fascinated by her new relatives. "Wow, you really look like her. I guess I do, too. She's dead now, right?"

"Yes," Bridget nodded. "A few years before Mom. We miss them both."

"You're so lucky, though. Growing up with all these people who loved you." Her face crumpled and tears filled her eyes. "I never did. Not that it's your fault, don't get me wrong. Everyone lied. To you, and to me."

"But, your grandparents must have loved you, honey. Look at all the trouble they went to, keeping your real relationship a secret. They protected you."

Lizzie grimaced. "Maybe. Or maybe they were protecting the family name. And the family money, of course."

"No, that can't be right." Bridget hadn't ever thought about it that way.

"They just wanted to be sure you couldn't take them to court, get custody, and come after the Longworth fortune." Lizzie's face looked hard and cold, unforgiving. "That's all anybody ever cared about. All my friends from school, their parents, everyone from the town where I grew up. They were so impressed, because my parents had tons of money and power. All the girls wanted to be invited to come spend the night, to see our house, swim in the pool and ride my pony. They didn't care at all about me, and I can prove it."

"What do you mean? How?"

Lizzie held out her left hand and wiggled the fingers. "Notice anything missing?" The diamond engagement ring was gone.

Bridget swallowed a gasp, shaking her head. "But I thought things were going so well?"

"They were, until he found out the truth. Stupid me, I blabbed the whole story. His parents had a fit, and two days later the wedding was officially cancelled." She sighed, shrugging her shoulders.

"You must know, he wasn't the right one." Bridget thought of her own failed marriages, each a testimony to the value of honesty in relationships. "If he truly loved you for who you are, there'd be no way anyone could talk him into calling it off. And that's the only kind of man who's good enough for you, my darling."

Lizzie raised her eyes with a bashful expression, her face blushing. "I know that's true, but it still hurts."

"I can see why." Bridget put her hand over Lizzie's and squeezed.

"Then the jerk went and told his sister, who told all my girlfriends, who now hate me. I'm not good enough for them anymore."

"Oh, no, I'm sure that's not true. It couldn't be."

Lizzie nodded. "It's true all right! We were all supposed to go skiing in Aspen for New Year's, but they disinvited me when Curtis broke it off. Said it would be too uncomfortable for him and nobody else would have any fun. And they stopped inviting me to ladies' night at our favorite bar in Boston, and nobody returns my texts."

"Oh honey, I'm so sorry. People can be incredibly nasty."

"Yeah." Lizzie stood up and wandered over to the tree. "This is beautiful. Did you make all these ornaments yourself?"

Bridget nodded. "I'm the queen of the hot glue gun and sparkly paint. Before I started my design business, I used to make things with shells and moss, stuff I found on the beach and in the woods. It's fun, and you'd be surprised how much people will pay for wall sconces made out of lichens."

"Really? I'm so impressed. Haven't got a creative bone in my body, except for writing. And nonfiction is my specialty." She went to the fireplace and leaned close, holding out her hands toward the flames. Lulu stretched and slid out of her bed, then asked to be petted by wagging her tail and winding herself around

Lizzie's ankles. "So, what's the program for tomorrow? Is your sister coming up, with her family?" She picked up the little dog and snuggled her close.

"Yes, but just for dinner in the afternoon. They're all going to Florida to visit her husband's parents, the day after. Everyone has to be packed and ready."

"I'm glad they'll be here. My troubles seem smaller, since I have a big new family to get to know. And, I'm glad they'll be leaving, too. It gives us the chance to spend some time alone together."

Bridget smiled. "Let's bring your things upstairs and get you settled, okay?"

"Okay."

Lizzie put down the dog and followed Bridget to the stairway, wheeling her suitcase behind her. She bumped it up the stairs and rolled it down the hallway, where her mother stood at the guest room door. It was cozy inside, and a jar candle flickered on the dresser. A wreath of sparkly pinecones decorated the window. "I see your glue gun has been at work in here too," she teased.

Bridget grinned. "You'll find clean towels in the bathroom, and extra blankets in the hall closet. Please ask if you need anything. Mom lived here on and off for forty years, so this house is well supplied. We even have snowshoes and cross-country skis, if you're so inclined."

"Wow, that sounds like fun. If it ever stops snowing so we can see where we're going." Lizzie peered out the window. "What is that across the street? Is it the lake?"

They stood side-by-side, looking outside into the blurry darkness as snowflakes tapped against the windowpanes. Across the street, a vast expanse of treeless white could be vaguely discerned.

"You need to see this view in the summer. It's fabulous." Bridget put her arm around Lizzie's shoulders.

"I'd love to." Her daughter looked at her. "You're so welcoming. It's awesome, really. That you'd just open up your life to a stranger like me."

"Lizzie, you aren't a stranger. You are part of me. I was so young, and I didn't handle it well. But now, here we are, together. It's a Christmas miracle."

They hugged again, and this time Bridget had a hard time letting go. But she held herself back, knowing that patience would be needed to grow the kind of intimacy that mothers and daughters share.

"Ready to turn in?"

Lizzie yawned and nodded. "It's been a long day. And driving in the snow is not my favorite thing."

"I'll go down and let the dogs out, then close up for the night." Bridget paused in the hallway. "You can have the bathroom first."

"Okay, cool."

"Welcome home, sweetheart. Sleep well."

Lizzie hugged herself, rubbing her arms. "It feels restful here. The cottage must be full of good memories. I'll sleep great!" She stepped forward and kissed Bridget carefully on the cheek. "Good night…Mom."

It was the word Bridget had waited to hear for what seemed like a lifetime, and the best Christmas present she could ever hope for.

Note: This scene follows the end of my bestselling novel, The Taste of Air *(2016, Red Adept Publishing). In book one, Bridget and Nell discover their mother Mary Reilly has been hiding a secret life for over forty years, with a lakeside cottage in Vermont and a set of complex relationships with people her daughters have never met. When the sisters delve into their mother's past, their own lives begin to unravel. Mary's hideaway is a vault for family secrets never suspected, and the gateway to change for all three women. (You can find this book at all major online booksellers) Bridget and Lizzie's story continues in the next book of the series,* The Scent of Earth. *Look for it in 2019.*

BOOKS BY GAIL

DESTINED, by Gail Cleare, 2011 (G&G Publications).
Magic Realism/Romance.
http://www.gailcleare.com/destined.html

THE TASTE OF AIR, 2016 (Red Adept Publishing),
USA Today Bestseller. Women's Fiction.
http://www.gailcleare.com/tasteofair.html

LOVE & CHOCOLATE, 2018 (Red Adept Publishing).
Romance,
http://www.gailcleare.com/lovechocolate.html

ABOUT GAIL

USA Today Bestselling author Gail Cleare used to write for newspapers, magazines, ad agencies, Fortune 50 companies and AOL. Now she writes fiction, and lives on an 18th century farm in Massachusetts with her family and dogs, cats, chickens, black bears, blue herons, rushing streams and wide, windy skies. When she's not writing, Gail is usually working in her organic vegetable garden or stalking wild creatures with a 300mm lens.

Cleare's debut novel is "Destined, a Novel of the Tarot"(2011), a magic realism romance. The audiobook, featuring narrator Marnye Young, will be released in 2018. Her second novel, *USA Today Bestseller* "The Taste of Air" (2016), is a womens' fiction family drama, and in 2017 it won Readers' Favorite awards for the book and the audiobook. "Love & Chocolate," a romance with recipes, is a romantic comedy to be released in the fall of 2018. It's the first volume of a trilogy featuring the Dumas family and their restaurant, The Three Chocolatiers.

For the latest news, visit gailcleare.com or Gail's Facebook page at facebook.com/GailCleareAuthor/. You can follow Gail on twitter @gcleare and on Bookbub at https://www.bookbub.com/authors/gail-cleare

SOME CARRY-TAIL: A GABRIEL & ORSON CHRISTMAS

BY VICTOR CATANO

I see the trick on't: here was a consent,
Knowing aforehand of our merriment,
To dash it like a Christmas comedy:
Some carry-tale, some please-man, some slight zany

Love's Labours Lost,
Act v Scene ii

I leaned against the low wall at Rockefeller Center, just above the ice rink and across from a massive tree with a million lights. I craned my neck to take in all forty feet as I sipped my coffee, nudged the chubby bulldog at my feet, and shared some of my trademark humor.

"That's one impressive bathroom."

The dog grunted. *Oh come on, Gabriel. Get new material.*

The thought scratched my brain, uninvited. The source of the thought was the same chubby brown and white bulldog who was vigorously scratching behind his ear.

Besides, you know I prefer fire hydrants.

"True enough, Orson. You're a city dog."

Orson belonged to my girlfriend, Sheila. She was a beautiful, funny woman with long, black hair that entranced me. She was also a witch. Orson was her familiar, an animal companion who helped her channel her magic. As a result, they could speak telepathically. And because Sheila and Orson had welcomed me into their pack, I could hear him as well.

Damn right. Now take me to Magnolia. I want a cupcake.

This had its downsides.

We threaded our way through the thousands of people jockeying for position at the base of the tree to get the perfect selfie. I had moved here after I was discharged from the army, so I lacked that natural talent the natives had for dodging oblivious tourists. Twice I'd been bumped by families rushing to the tree and twice I'd almost dumped hot coffee on toddlers. Orson waddled on through without incident.

I'm stealthy. Like a ninja.

I saw a lot of kung fu movies on Saturday afternoon TV growing up. Most of the ninjas I saw were a little more agile. And probably farted less.

We made it to the corner and saw the line for Magnolia cupcakes stretched halfway down the block. Orson whined piteously.

"Hey you wanted Magnolia, not me. *Sex and the City* has brainwashed everyone."

Sheila loved the show and Orson cuddled up on her lap while she watched the reruns on HBO. Obviously, he cared more about snacks than Carrie's romantic life. Orson was *such* a Miranda.

Still, he wanted a cupcake. We settled into the line that started back by the NBC Store. I tried to pass the time with some subtle chit-chat.

"So… You gonna tell me what Mama wants for Christmas?"

Orson grunted. *No.*

"Oh come on. You know I'm terrible at gifts."

Yeah, I know. You got me a cat *toy last year.*

I threw up my hands in exasperation. "It was a squeaky bird! You like squeaky birds! You chewed up three of them last year."

It had catnip! You don't give a dog catnip!

"You're just proving my point! I'm bad at gifts, so just tell me what Sheila wants."

No, Mama made me promise. I started to roll my eyes, but Orson cut me off. *She said that you'd know what to get her.*

This was terrible advice. Sheila was beautiful and smart and (literally) magical. I had my moments, but I was definitely at a disadvantage to her in all three areas.

We finally made our way up to the counter of the cupcake store. Orson was practically drooling on the display case, and his hungry panting was steaming up the glass. Even though there were plenty of "Service Animals Only" signs, Orson had no problem getting in. He always said that he provided a valuable service by being so handsome. Sheila would roll her eyes at this, and say it was more about magical shielding. She said it wasn't so much "invisibility" as it was making people not notice you.

After some hard decisions, we walked out of the bakery with a box of four cupcakes for me and Sheila and a lemon buttercream cupcake for Orson. He bounced excitedly as we made our way back to the edge of the rink. I peeled the foil back from the cupcake and set it down in front of Orson. He was bouncing in place, drool spattering at my feet.

Yes! Yes! Mama never lets me have one! He chomped down on the frosting and practically rolled his eyes back in ecstasy.

"So is that better than a catnip bird?"

Yes. You're forgiven.

I was about to ask for a hint about what to get Sheila, when a man with a vacant stare staggered toward us. His jacket was open and in spite of the cold, sweat trickled down his brow.

There was something about that dazed look. I'd seen it before.

The man lurched through the crowds, not paying any attention to his surroundings. I took a step back to avoid him plowing into me. Orson didn't notice him until he tromped his foot two inches from the dwindling pile of icing and crumbs.

Orson growled. *Hey! Watch it! He almost stepped on my cupcake!*

The growl startled the man out of his daze. He let out a yelp and backed into the wall around the ice rink. He pinwheeled his arms, afraid he was going to tumble over.

I grabbed his coat to steady him. "Hey, take it easy pal! The dog won't hurt you. He was just mad you almost stepped on his treat."

Orson kept on growling. *I am not standing in that line again.*

The sweaty man shifted his gaze between Orson and me until he finally seemed to realize what was happening. "Sorry! I'm sorry! Look, I didn't realize I stepped too close, it's just..ah…well…"

I let go of his coat and nudged Orson back with my foot. "Don't worry about it." A bead of sweat dropped on my hand. "Hey buddy, are you all right? Are you having a stroke?"

He tried to relax his shoulders and straighten up. "No, no, nothing like that. It's just…" He looked past my head and locked eyes on something.

I turned slightly to see an adorable little girl in pigtails and a navy blue felt coat skipping towards us smiling. I guessed she was about seven or eight. This had to be his daughter, but Dad wasn't happy. He was petrified.

That triggered a childhood memory. My dad, sweaty and evasive, trying to avoid answering direct questions, stumbling around dazed. He had bet a bundle on Florida in a college football game. The Gators got pummeled. I also remembered getting a pack of gum for Christmas that year and Dad telling me it must've been because I was bad and Santa saw it.

I clamped onto the man's shoulder. "Nothing like what? Like leaving your kid alone in Manhattan so you could blow your Christmas fund doing something stupid?"

His eyes popped wide with alarm and his mouth made a little 'o' as he tried to think up a lie.

The voice behind me squeaked. "Daddy! There you are! I was looking at the tree, but I didn't see you. I was getting worried." She saw my arm on his shoulder. "Who's this?" She sounded a little nervous.

There's no way I'd ever frighten a kid, especially a week before Christmas. I put on my best smile and squatted down to be on her level. "Hi sweetie! My name is Gabriel. And this handsome fellow is Orson." Orson waddled over and rubbed his head on her leg. She giggled. "I'm a friend of your Dad's from way back. I'm sorry to make him late but I hadn't seen him in ages."

I offered her my hand and she shook it. She had on thin dollar store gloves that had a couple of holes in them. Her skin felt chilly through the fabric. She then turned to her dad. "Did you see Santa? Did you tell him? Did you tell him I want a pretty dolly with red hair?" She turned to me to explain. "I asked Daddy to go see Santa for me. I get all nervous and forget what I want to ask him for, so I made Daddy go because he's all smart and I know he won't forget and I really want a new dolly." Barely pausing for air, she spun back to Daddy. "So did you tell him?"

Now Dad was sweating so much I thought he'd pass out. "Um, well... I went to see him, but, uh... I don't think he heard everything I said... It was kind of loud, and..."

Oh no, what did you do? I nodded to Orson and jerked my head away from the edge of the rink. "Hey, sweetheart? Do you like my doggie, Orson?" She nodded and grinned.

Orson gave her a toothy smile. *Of course she does! She has good taste.*

"Can you do me a favor? He really wants to go sniff that tree over there." I pointed to the Christmas tree. ""Would you mind walking over while I chat with your dad?"

Sniff a tree? Is that the best you could come up with? Orson rolled his eyes but played along, nudging her towards the tree. Orson's little tail started wagging vigorously as they walked away.

I spun the guy to face me. "Ok, you've got ten seconds to explain what you did with the Christmas money."

He tried to play innocent. "What? I didn't—"

I cut him off. "Oh stop it. I know that look. My dad had that look every other weekend when he'd lose all his money on a football game. So what happened?"

His shoulders slumped. "I lost it to Santa."

"What?"

"Two blocks from here. He was playing Three-card Monte."

Of all the stupid… Every turnip truck tourist knows that Three-card Monte's a scam. Except for this guy, apparently. "You got hustled by Santa Claus."

He shrugged sadly. "He got all my money. Now I can't get Jenny that doll."

I shook my head. "Come on, let's go."

"Where?"

I waved at Orson, who galumphed his way back to me, Jenny close behind. "Take me to this Santa Claus. If that game is still running, I'm getting your money back."

A couple blocks south on 46th the stores were less flashy, although the rents were still sky high. In front of a vacant storefront with a prominently displayed "For Lease" sign, a small crowd was clumped around a grungy Santa Claus hunched over a cardboard box. The man smiled, but didn't look particularly jolly. His tummy twitched more than shook and it wasn't like jelly, more like a bag of jumpy spiders. He looked like a tweaker who'd boosted a coat off a Salvation Army Santa twice his size.

The only thing on him that didn't shake were his fingers. They steadily flew over three bent cards on the box as he shuffled them around.

I glanced over at the schlub I was trying to help. "What's your name again?"

"Jerry."

I groaned. "Jerry, Three-card Monte's a scam. Don't they have televisions in Iowa or wherever the hell you're from?"

"New Jersey. But it looked so easy!" Jerry whined. "I mean, the guy before me won a hundred bucks! I just wanted to be able to afford something nice for Jenny."

Sure he did. It was all I could do not to grind my teeth to stubs. "How much did you lose?"

Jerry got very interested in his shoes. "One fifty." I was about to yell at him but he interrupted me. "It all happened so fast! I was down forty and then I tried to get it back and in two minutes I was broke."

Orson growled. *Remind me why we're helping this cupcake-stomping jerk.*

Jenny stepped in front of us and squinted across the street. She frowned. "That doesn't look like Santa to me."

Good eye, kid. "It isn't." I said. "It's one of his junior assistants in training."

"Oh. Daddy, no wonder he didn't hear you!"

God bless the eternally forgiving nature of children. "Jenny, you stay here with your Dad. I am going to go see if we can talk to his supervisor."

We jogged across the street. Well, I jogged. Orson trundled.

Twitchy Claus was shuffling his cards and he had the patter going. "Find the red queen! Find the red queen! So easy! So easy! Highest bet gets all the money!"

A black kid in a North Face parka plunked down a twenty. Twitchy went through his shuffle, floating the cards back and forth at lightning speed. North Face pointed at the card on the right and the dealer turned over the Queen of Hearts. The kid pumped his fist and took his winnings.

Twitchy shouted at the crowd. "Just that easy and you could be a winner! Who wants to try their luck?"

Orson grunted. *He's in on it.*

"Of course he is." I whispered. "His only job is to lure in the suckers. And if someone manages to pick the right card by chance, he comes in with a higher bet so the sucker still doesn't win."

So how are we going to?

I gave him a winning smile. "Who said we were going to play fair?"

Gotcha. And work on that smile. It looks weird.

I walked up to the table. "Well, this looks like fun!"

Twitchy Claus smiled, a feral glint in his eye. "Lots of fun! Don't have to go all the way to Foxwoods to win big money! You in?"

"Sure!" I reached into my pocket and pulled out some bills. I put ten bucks on the table.

Twitchy shook me off. "Come on, man. I thought you wanted to make some *money*. Don't throw no chicken feed down."

I hemmed and hawed, then put down another twenty.

"That's more like it! All right! Here we go!" His hands flashed across the table. He'd done this a while and I didn't even try to follow them.

I left that to Orson.

Orson stared at the cards as they zipped back and forth. Then Twitchy stopped and spread his hands out.

Center.. Orson's eyes had little gold flecks in them. They sparked anytime he "talked" to Sheila. They sparked now.

I pointed at the center card. He smiled and flipped it over. Six of Clubs.

"Sorry, man! You gotta keep your eyes on the cards!"

Hey! That was the Queen! I know it.

I knew it too. He'd slipped a card out from his big Santa sleeve when he flipped it. I only saw because I was looking for it instead of staring at the cards.

"Aw, man! I could've sworn that was it!" I reached into my pocket and pulled out fifty. "Let's try that again!"

Again, he flipped and moved the cards around the table. Again, Orson followed the cards. *Left!* This time, instead of pointing at the card, I put my finger on top of it.

"This one! I'll flip it!"

Twitchy Claus swallowed hard and fake-coughed twice. The North Face kid put a hundred on the board. Twitchy nodded at the c-note. "Sorry, gotta take highest bet." North Face pointed left, and - whaddaya know! - it was the Queen.

I put my hands on my hips. "Darn it! That was my win! One more round." I pulled out $300. "This time, for sure!"

Twitchy was practically drooling. Once more the shuffle. *Center!* Once more, I put my finger on the card so Santa couldn't swap it out. Once more, North Face walked to the table. At least he tried to. Orson bit his pant leg and tripped him. The kid hit the ground hard and didn't try to get up.

I smiled at Twitchy. "No more bets. I'm gonna flip this over." I did. And there was the red queen. "Yes!" I pumped my fist in victory.

Twitchy's eyes were darting back and forth, looking for an exit and getting ready to sprint. He took one step and ran into Orson doing his best Cujo imitation. He barked and snapped and got a lot of drool on Santa's jeans and ratty sneakers.

"Hey, where you going? You almost forgot to pay me!" I blinked my eyes innocently.

Faced with a snarling dog and an unconscious associate, he slowly reached into his coat and brought out $300.

"Thank you, kind sir! Merry Christmas!"

I trotted across the street, with Orson on my heels. I heard Twitchy start to yell something at me just as a patrol car turned the corner. It whooped the siren once, and Twitchy decided it was better to run away than to spend a night in Rikers.

Jerry's eyes lit up when he saw the money we'd won. "You did it! You got it back for me!"

I glared at him. "I didn't do it for you."

He looked confused for a second then remembered. "Right, right." He held out his hand expectantly. I just stared at it. "Hey, come on, man. I need to do my Christmas shopping."

I narrowed my eyes. "You can't get her the present she needs most, namely a better father. And I don't trust you to walk fifteen feet without spending this on magic beans."

He started to protest, but I moved toward Jenny and Orson. She was beaming and giving Orson tummy rubs. He licked her face appreciatively. Thank goodness the last thing he'd eaten was a cupcake.

"Good news! I talked to Santa for you and gave him your list!"

Jenny clapped her hands joyfully. "Thank you! Is he going to get me my dolly?"

"Even better! He told me that he and the elves were going to be so busy that we should go and get it right now. He gave me money from Mrs. Claus so we can go shopping."

Jenny looked concerned. "I don't think that's how it works."

I gave her my most cheerful smile. "Hey, Santa himself said it was OK. He wanted you to pick the dolly that you love the most."

Orson chuffed. *Oof. Tone it down. This ain't a Crest commercial and your smile is frightening me.*

We walked to the *American Girl* store. It was teeming with young girls, excited to spend a wad of their parent's money on a doll with a historical backstory. Jenny picked one from the Revolutionary War era, but I think her choice had more to do with the fact that it had red hair. Jenny bounced up and down while the cheerfully tired clerk wrapped up her purchase. Orson sat by my feet and scratched his ear.

I took that moment to lean in to Jerry. "Now listen. You and your daughter will go back to Jersey and have a lovely Christmas. Take the rest of the money and get that poor wife of yours something nice. And if I ever hear that you're in my city again and falling for sucker scams, I will track you down and kick your ass up and down Broadway."

Jerry thought that would be a great time to show a little spine. Jerry was not a bright man. "Hey, no one tells me what to-"

I put my arm across his shoulders to disguise me Vulcan-nerve-pinching his neck. "Yeah, I think that's the problem. You don't listen when people tell you things. Did it occur to you how I beat that Three-card Monte game? It wasn't luck. I had…special ways."

I looked down at Orson, Jerry followed with his eyes. Fortunately, Orson had heard and stopped scratching. He was always good at improv. His eyes glowed golden and he added a low growl.

Jerry gasped and squirmed, but I had a good grip. "So get this straight. We will know if you come back. And God help you if you screw up like this again."

I released my pinch. Jerry slumped, but I propped him back up as Jenny turned around.

"I got it! Thank you for going to see Santa, Daddy!" She gave Orson a big hug. "And Merry Christmas to you, doggy!"

Orson panted happily. *Make her leave! I can't keep up my jaded New Yorker front when little kids are hugging me.*

She skipped out the door, giving me a chance to say goodbye to my new best friend, Jerry. "That girl thinks the world of you. Don't disappoint her again." Orson growled for emphasis. Jerry nodded and scurried out the door.

Orson and I ambled out into the bustling crowds. *That was nice of you.*

I shrugged "I had too many terrible Christmases as a kid. I couldn't stand to see a dirtbag like that give one to his kid."

Orson scratched himself. *She'll find out her Dad's a creep soon enough.*

I looked across the street at a bell-ringing Santa collecting for the Salvation Army. "Yeah, but for a little while longer, her Dad's still a good guy. And this will always be the Christmas that Santa Claus bought her a doll in New York. With an assist from Orson the Elf."

Ho ho ho.

"Come on. We need to get home to Sheila. And you need to tell me what she wants for Christmas."

Orson waddled ahead of me. *Don't worry. I think you're doing great so far.*

THE END

BOOKS BY VICTOR

You can read more about Gabriel & Orson in their debut novel,
Tail & Trouble. Volume Two,
The Winter of Our Distemper
https://www.goodreads.com/book/show/28575361-tail-trouble

ABOUT VICTOR

Victor Catano lives in New York City with his wonderful wife, Kim, and their pughuahua, Danerys. When not writing, he works in live theater as a stage manager, light designer, and technical director, working mainly with dance companies. His hobbies include coffee, Broadway musicals, and complaining about the NY Mets and Philadelphia Eagles. (Well, less about the Eagles these days.)

GET IN TOUCH

Official Facebook: facebook.com/VictorCatanoAuthor
Website: VictorCatanoAuthor.weebly.com
Twitter: twitter.com/VGCatano
Instagram: Instagram.com/vgcatano
Bookbub: www.bookbub.com/authors/victor-catano
Goodreads: www.goodreads.com/author/show/14873908.Victor_Catano

A Twin Oaks Christmas

BY REECE TAYLOR

Hannah

"Hannah, why don't you go meet the guys and I'll finish packing these up. MaCee is on her way and can help me bring them to town." Lee pushes me toward the door.

Looking back at all the baked goods covering every surface of our house, I try to resist. "Lee there's so much. I can't leave you with this mess."

"Angel, it's fine. MaCee will help, and I'll call Toby if I need to. We'll take care of it. Go, or they'll be sitting there waiting on you."

I finally give up the argument, leaving him to it.

The Twin Oaks Christmas Parade and Festival is today, and the town is bustling with activity. I have been recruited to judge the window decorating contest, along with Sawyer Wilks and Tyler Dixon. We're supposed to be meeting in fifteen minutes, but with all the cookies, pies, and cakes I've been baking all day, I am running late.

MaCee, Toby, and I volunteered to set up a booth with Christmas goodies and donate the proceeds to the town charity that helps underprivileged families in our community. It's a great cause and should really help, but right now, it's stressing me out.

Tyler and Sawyer are standing on the corner of Main Street when I arrive. Tyler looks at his watch as I rush up slightly out of breath.

"So sorry, guys. I was p`utting the final touches on a cake and time got away from me," I reach into my bag and take out a notebook and pen. "I've written down all the names of the businesses participating, and I even made columns for the items we are judging. We have creativity, Christmas theme, and overall appearance."

"Wow, girl, aren't you organized. I'm glad you thought to do that. I was at a loss as to how we were going to judge this thing," Sawyer compliments, looking at my list.

"And that is why we have Hannah. She's here to keep us straight."

Blushing at Tyler's comment, I turn to lead the men to our first contestant.

The window of The Baked Oak is decorated with Santa holding a cake and several elves surrounding him with cupcakes in their hands. After scoring it, we continue down the street to each window until we reach The Twisted Oak.

Surprising as it is, Mitchell has outdone himself. I had no idea he was such a good artist. He's decorated his window with a reindeer sitting on top of an old lady and Santa holding his face in his hands, with several other reindeer standing around laughing.

"Mitchell did a great job. I saw him out here working on it but had no idea it would turn out this good." Sawyer laughs.

Tyler and I agree. The window is creative, funny and has a Christmas theme.

Sawyer's window has Santa getting a tattoo of Jingle Bells. I want to nominate it, but he feels we shouldn't be participating since we are judging the contest.

The window at The Handy Oak has Santa putting up Christmas lights, with Mrs. Claus directing him and the elves tangled in the lights.

I love all the decorations, and everyone seems to have had a great time doing them—except for Mr. Joey Thompson.

He participated, but it looks like it was a struggle. The Drunken Oak has a hand drawn stick figure with a Santa hat in their window. The figure is holding a bottle of wine and the words "Bah humbug" are written underneath it. I felt bad giving him zero points, so he got a one under participation and a one under creativity. Tyler and Sawyer are standing in front of the drawing and contemplating it as if looking at a masterpiece until Sawyer can't keep a straight face any longer and they both start laughing.

"Gotta love Mr. Joey. He does things his way," Sawyer says as we walk across the street to The Floating Oak, DeeDee Duncan's shop. Miss DeeDee is our resident hippy and her window reflects this. It has a woman in a flowy dress riding a unicorn surrounded by clouds. The woman is throwing presents to children below her.

"Is the unicorn farting holly berries and leaves?" I move closer to get a better look.

"Those holly leaves look suspiciously like marijuana leaves, if you ask me." Laughing, Tyler takes the scoresheet and marks a three for creativity.

"Everyone did a great job, and I have a feeling this is going to become a tradition around town," Tyler says.

Sawyer takes my notebook and adds up all the scores. "Looks like Mitchell at The Twisted Oak is our winner, and The Handy Oak is our runner up."

Retrieving the pad from Sawyer, I stick it back in my bag. "I'm going to take our results to the mayor and will see y'all at the festival."

The mayor has a booth set up at the gazebo in the middle of the park. After handing her the results, I walk over to our booth of baked goods to help MaCee, Toby, and Lee put the finishing touches on it. Minutes before the parade is due to start, we walk over to the route to watch.

Most of the town businesses have floats in the parade, and everyone is throwing candy, beads, and toys to the bystanders. Can't have a parade in Louisiana and not throw a few beads.

Laughing, MaCee points down the street at Santa's float. "Holy Cow! Now *that's* a float."

Mrs. Ruby Thompson and Miss DeeDee must have designed it, and it's a doozy. They have Mr. Joey Thompson sitting on a golden throne while the two ladies fan him. Wearing a Santa suit and a large, fake beard, the scowl on his face does not say "happy." The float is covered in a white, fluffy material that is supposed to look like snow, and decorated trees are scattered around the space. There are several children dressed as elves and reindeer throwing candy and beads.

The float stops at the park entrance, and Mitchell jumps out of the truck. Grabbing some wooden stairs, he sets them on the side of the trailer for the occupants to exit. The elves and reindeer step off first and form two lines with an aisle down the center.

"Santa! Santa! All hail the great Santa!" they chant, and one lone voice yells, "Dilly, Dilly!"

I laugh when Mr. Joey can't hide his grin at Rowdy Wilks.

Ruby and DeeDee exit next and scatter holly and poinsettia leaves on the ground for Mr. Joey to walk upon. It's a very comical sight, and if looks could kill, I believe both women would be in danger. Mr. Joey had nominated the ladies as his helpers to get revenge for them nominating him as Santa, but I believe they turned the tables on him. They embraced their "slave" status and are putting on quite the show.

Santa makes his way to the chair set up near the gazebo and takes a seat. If I'm not mistaken, I heard him mumbling something about putting coals in a couple ladies' stockings.

Mr. Joey plasters a fake smile on his face that soon becomes real when the first child, a small girl, grins up at him and gives him a hug after he hands her a doll.

"Aw … Look at Mr. Cranky Pants. His heart melted like a snowball in New Orleans," Toby remarks.

Laughing, we agree with Toby as the children crowd around Mr. Joey.

We walk over to open our booth, where Lee and MaCee have all the goods arranged and even have sold signs on a couple of the cakes. I catch Toby sneaking a couple cookies and pat his hand.

"Hey, I'm planning on paying for them. You know, it's rude to slap the customers," he admonishes, and I hold my hand out for his cash.

"The Santa float is one for the record books. I don't think I've ever seen Santa presented as a king."

Agreeing with MaCee, I laugh and wonder how Ruby convinced him to do it.

"It was definitely a new take on things. Mr. Joey looked fit to be tied," Lee adds.

Working at the booth for only a few hours, we sell all our goods and close shop, making quite a bit for the charity. After giving our proceeds to the committee, we join the rest of the town for caroling. Squeezing between Lee and MaCee, I lip sync each song—my singing is no match for them. They sound amazing, and several folks stop singing to listen to them. Lee and MaCee look around, confusion on their faces, and finally get quiet.

"No, keep singing. You two sound so good together." Lee blushes at Mrs. Carlston's compliment but turns to MaCee and they continue.

Eggnog and spiced holiday punch is in abundance following the caroling session. The mayor announces the winners of the window decorating contest, and Mitchell acts as though he has won an Oscar.

"I would like to thank my family for all your support and the judges for being able to recognize true talent. Most of all, thank you to my loyal fans. Without you, I would never have come this far." Mitchell holds his trophy in the air as everyone cheers.

"I had no idea Mitchell was so comical. The mayor looks as though she wants to smack him," Toby says.

We all look at the stage just as the mayor shoves him aside and steps up to the microphone.

"I would like to thank everyone who participated in today's festivities. We made over ten thousand dollars for our Christmas fund. This will go a long way in helping families in our community have a wonderful holiday."

This is the first town event Lee and I have attended as a couple, and I'm happier than I have ever been. Today is a prelude to how wonderful our lives are going to be in Twin Oaks.

Lee

"Do you know those folks over there?" I nudge Hannah and point to a family standing off to the side by themselves.

"No, I've never seen them before. Let's go check it out." Hannah grabs my hand and leads me toward them.

I live for this girl. We're going to my mother's for dinner soon, and MaCee and her husband Tyler are joining us. I'm looking forward to having our family together.

"Hi, I'm Hannah Dale, and this is Lee Burkett, my fiancé. Y'all look a bit lost. Can we help you with anything?" She extends her hand for the woman to shake.

"Thank you so much. I'm Susan Howard, and this is my husband Rodney. Rodney's mother lived her a long time ago and passed away two months ago. Her last wish was for us to reconnect with her sister. We think she might still live here."

"Who is your aunt? We may know her," I offer.

"Mrs. Sally Arceneaux, she was my mother's oldest sister," Rodney replies.

I raise a brow. "I know Miss Sally. I didn't know she had family."

"She's sitting over there." Hannah points into the crowd.

Rodney looks over and stares for a moment. "Wow, I would have known her anywhere. It's uncanny how much she looks like my mother."

"Where are y'all from? Your accent is British. Do you live in the States?" Hannah is the only person I know who can ask a stranger a personal question and they won't take offense.

"No, we don't live in the States, we're from Bristol, England. It's been a long journey. I only hope she wants to see us." Susan hugs her two children to her.

A boy and a girl, they look to be around eight and ten respectively. Both are smiling and looking at the townspeople in awe.

The girl tugs on her mother's hand and looks up at her. "Can we go see Santa?"

"No, dear, we aren't from here. It would be rude to impose."

I shake my head. "No, ma'am, you're in the South. We treat everyone like family. She's more than welcome to go see Santa. You and Hannah can take the children while I walk with Rodney to meet Miss Sally."

Rodney smiles at my suggestion and looks relieved to be meeting her without the children present.

"Thank you so much for that," Rodney says as we head toward his aunt. "I was trying to figure out a way to meet her on my own. She and my mother had a falling out years ago, and Mother worried she would not be very accepting of us. I must admit I'm a bit nervous."

As we approach her, Miss Sally laughs at Mr. Joey who's acting jolly when everyone knows jolly is not his forte. Rodney and I stand awkwardly for a moment before I clear my throat.

"Miss Sally? I have someone here to see you."

She looks up at us with surprise and hops out of her chair to grab Rodney in a bear hug. He stands with his arms akimbo for a few seconds before returning her hug with tears in his eyes. I step away to give them some privacy.

"Rodney? Oh, my boy Rodney. I never thought I would see you." She holds him back at arm's length and eyes him up and down. "Let me look at you. What a fine man you turned out to be. What are you doing here?"

"I can't believe you know who I am. I was so nervous you wouldn't believe me or wouldn't want anything to do with us," Rodney says, smiling from ear to ear.

"Your mother was my baby sister, and even though we didn't see eye to eye, I still loved her." Miss Sally stops and takes a deep breath. "I will always regret not reaching out to her to mend our fences after our disagreement. I kept tabs on her though. Your dad wrote me letters for years and kept me updated on your lives. He tried telling her, but she became so angry with him, he kept it from her. Once the internet came around, I found you online. I am sorry about your mother's death. I know she loved you."

Rodney wraps his arms around Miss Sally and gives her another hug. "Mum wanted us to reconnect with you. It was her dying wish. She regretted being so stubborn and, in the end, became too weak to travel and make amends."

Tears stream down Miss Sally's face, and we've drawn the attention of several onlookers. Mr. Hanks, the owner of The Handy Oak, walks over and puts his arm around Miss Sally's shoulders. She straightens and takes a deep breath, getting hold of her emotions.

"Everyone, I would like to introduce you to my nephew, Rodney Howard. He is here all the way from England, and I couldn't be happier to see him," Miss Sally announces to the crowd.

People approach Rodney and welcome him to the town. Shaking their hands, he looks a bit dumbstruck by the overwhelming inclusion of the town.

Miss Sally gushes over the children when his family joins the group, and she invites them to stay with her. I overhear Rodney and Susan make the decision to stick around for Christmas.

"Oh, Lee, this is so wonderful. I've always worried about Miss Sally. She's had no one, and my family has invited her to dinner on several holidays only to be shot down. She gets offended when she thinks people are offering charity. Still, I hate for anyone to be alone during Christmastime." Hannah has such a tender heart.

Hugging her close, I kiss her forehead. "Angel, it looks like everyone is going to have a Merry Christmas this year, even Twin Oaks' grumpy Santa looks happy."

Mr. Joey has a toddler on his shoulders and a little girl on his knee. The man looks like he's in heaven as he laughs at something one of the children says.

The mayor taps the microphone a couple of times to get everyone's attention. "I would like to welcome the Howard family to Twin Oaks." Claps and cheers follow her announcement. "I am officially declaring the end of the Christmas Festival. Merry Christmas, everyone!"

BOOKS BY REECE

TWIN OAKS SERIES

Mama Knows Best

Bless Your Heart

Chin Up Buttercup (coming soon)

ABOUT REECE

Reece has always been an avid listener to people's stories and has loved telling some of her own. When she became a teenager, her grandmother gave her a romance novel (very G-rated) and this began her love of reading. She has dabbled with writing for years and never committed to just doing it. Finally, she made up her mind and decided to try due to the fact there were so many stories in her mind that wanted out. She lives at the beach with her husband and dog in Alabama.

GET IN TOUCH

Website: www.reecetaylorwrites.com
Facebook: https://www.facebook.com/AuthorReeceTaylor
Instagram: @authorreecetaylor
Twitter: @readreecetaylor

The Christmas Jacket

BY DIANE BYINGTON

E very Christmas is magical in its way, but the Christmas I want to tell you about happened in 1967, when I was fifteen. My parents and I had moved from Ohio to a small town in the center of Florida—Valencia—three months before. We were poor, and my dad drank, so Christmas wasn't going to be much at our house. In fact, if I hadn't thrown a fit, we wouldn't have even had a Charlie Brown Christmas tree that year. My dad was a migrant farm worker and my mom cooked and took care of the old couple who lived in the big house on their farm, while we lived in the tiny cottage beside it. For my parents, Christmas was just a day when they didn't have to work. Mom usually spent it watching sappy Christmas movies on television and Dad would play whiny songs on his guitar and drink beer.

This was going to be a different kind of Christmas for me. For one thing, I'd always experienced snow on Christmas. I knew it wouldn't snow that far south, but Christmas day was forecast to be cold. It would have to do. But hanging Christmas lights on palm trees just felt… wrong.

Because money was so tight, Mom didn't bother to ask what I wanted for Christmas, and I didn't offer. I figured I would get something small, as usual. I hoped for a record album or a book, maybe even a sweater, but that was about all I could expect.

I didn't dare ask for it, but I was dying for a Valencia High athletic jacket. The jacket was maroon and white and was just the right weight to keep me warm without being too heavy, and it had the school's name embroidered on the back. Some of the athletes also had letters sewn on the front. I was on the track team, but I hadn't been running long enough to earn a letter. Even though my parents didn't approve of my running (that's another story), I was an athlete and I wanted to prove it by wearing one of those jackets. The problem was that they cost $25, which was a lot of money in those days and always would be for poor people like us. I knew I wouldn't get one, so there was no use whining about it. "No use whining about it" was a standard phrase in our house, attributed to everything from store-bought clothes to staying in one place long enough to finish out the school year.

I planned to give my parents a pelican I had carved from cypress wood during the slow days at my after-school job. My friend Francie's Uncle Stan owned the store where I worked, and he had taught me how to carve—sort of. It was my first effort, and I hoped my parents would take that into consideration when they unwrapped it.

On Christmas morning, I woke up early and tiptoed into the living room. "Santa" had left a few things beneath the tree. A quick glance at the shape of the boxes told me I had guessed right. Record, book, probably sweater. I'd open the gifts later, and ooh and ahh over them, but first I wanted to go for a run. I dressed in my usual shorts and tee-shirt but realized my mistake as soon as I walked outside. *Brrr.* Too cold for those clothes. Back inside, I pulled on sweat pants, but I didn't have the right weight jacket. My winter coat was too heavy. What to do? Rummaging through my closet, I found a wool sweater that I'd worn when we lived in Ohio. Moths had eaten holes all over it, so it wasn't fit to wear in public, but it might work for running.

Francie, my running partner and friend, lived a half mile away. I was surprised to see her stretching outside her house when I ran by. "Merry Christmas," I said, running up to her, "I thought you wouldn't be able to run today."

"Hi, Faye. Merry Christmas to you, too. Mom told me to be back in half an hour to start cooking, so I've only got a little while." She peered at me. "What is that you're wearing?"

I felt myself blush. Francie's family was rich. She wouldn't be caught dead wearing a holey sweater. "I know. Ugly. But it'll keep me warm. Come on, let's go."

We ran into town and back. When we returned to her house, Francie said, "Come in for a minute. I want to show you something."

"All right."

She led me into her bedroom and stopped before a large bag that appeared to be filled with clothes. "Mom had Kyle and me go through all our clothes and pick out a bunch of stuff to give to a Cambodian refugee family that are new here. They had to leave their country so fast that they couldn't take anything. Can you imagine? Anyway, I wondered if you wanted to go through it and take what you want before we give it to them." She shrugged. "Mom said it would be okay."

I wasn't sure what to say. Francie's parents were so nice that I didn't think about them being rich very often. Francie and I were about the same size, so her castoffs would be better than my best clothes. But was it the right thing to do?

I was about to decline when I noticed, on top of the bag, what looked like a Valencia High jacket. I couldn't help myself. I walked over to it and picked it up. *Yep.* I hadn't even told Francie how much I wanted one of those.

"You getting rid of this?" I asked, trying to sound casual.

"Not me. It's Kyle's. Now that he's in college, he doesn't want stuff that reminds him of high school." She shook her head. "You're welcome to it."

Oh, gosh. I had only met Francie's brother once before, at their house a couple of months earlier. But he was the cutest boy I'd ever seen and I had a huge crush on him. Now I doubly wanted it. It might smell like Kyle, and I could pretend I was his girlfriend when I wore it. And everybody would know I was an athlete. I'd be warm, too. The jacket was perfect.

But how could I possibly accept this gift? My mom constantly harped that we didn't take charity. Sure, we shopped at Goodwill all the time, but that wasn't charity, she said. It was just smart shopping.

But oh, how I wanted that jacket. I said, "Are you sure it's okay to take this? What about the Cambodian family? Won't one of them want it?"

"I don't know. Mom said I could give you first dibs. There's a couple of other jackets in there, too." She hesitated, as though she was thinking about saying something else. Finally, she said, "I think you should take it. Call it a Christmas present from Santa."

We laughed. I'd stopped believing in Santa at least ten years before.

"All right. Thank Kyle for me, okay?" I peeled off the holey sweater and dropped it on the floor. "Will you throw that away?" When Francie nodded, I slipped on the jacket and twirled in front of her mirror. It was a size too large, but that felt exactly right. The jacket's arms went past my hands, which would be great when it was cold. And it was long enough to cover my tee-shirts. I would be toasty warm without sweating. The deep maroon color even set off the highlights in my red hair. I held it up to my nose and sniffed. It smelled a little like pine needles. Probably not Kyle's smell, then. It must have been recently dry-cleaned.

I hugged Francie then walked home, luxuriating in my good fortune. Even though I didn't believe in him, Santa had definitely visited me that day.

Mom was making breakfast when I got home. She looked at me with that squinty expression I dreaded. "Where'd you get that jacket?"

I was stuck. If I said it was an old one of Kyle's, Mom would tell me I couldn't take charity and make me give it back. If I said Francie had given it to me, she would tell me it was too expensive and make me give it back. As I saw it, I had no choice but to lie. My mind worked feverishly. Finally, I said, "Francie loaned it to me. I didn't realize how cold it was outside."

She nodded. "That's sweet of her." Turning back to the griddle, she said, "Pancakes will be ready in a couple minutes. Wash your hands and set the table, will you?"

I felt bad about lying to my mom, especially on Christmas. But I wanted—needed—that jacket. I hung it up in my closet and ran my hand down the sleeves. The fabric was so soft that I wanted to rub my cheek on it. I would take the jacket to school and leave it there, so Mom would never know that I hadn't returned it.

We ate pancakes and opened our gifts. Just as I'd thought, I got a Beatles album, a Nancy Drew book that I'd read years before, and a pretty green sweater. I hugged my parents and told them to thank Santa for me. It was a longstanding joke in my family that Santa brought the gifts, so if I didn't like something I was supposed to blame Santa, not them. They meant well, and I was far mellower about everything since I had that jacket.

They unwrapped the bird. Dad said, "It's a pelican, right? Nice." I was so relieved that I nearly cried when he recognized what it was and liked it. Dad was usually either working or drunk, so he rarely paid any attention to me. At least so far, he was neither, so it was a good day.

I washed the dishes then went to my room to listen to my album while my parents read the newspaper. Afterward, we ate lunch and got ready to go to Francie's house. We'd been invited to join their family for dessert.

Kyle barely noticed my existence, because he was hanging out with his girlfriend, Linda, who turned out to be charming. I tried not to show my disappointment. Francie's dad and her Uncle Stan told stories about the war. They had been best buds all their lives and had been army pilots together. They'd gotten shot down and captured by the Germans. The ordeal had made them even closer friends. The whole afternoon was like a Norman Rockwell painting. Except that Dad got drunk, told off-color jokes, and embarrassed everybody. Same old, same old. Mom took him home early, but she allowed me to stay at Francie's for a while. After they left, Francie's mom, Laney, pulled me into the kitchen, just the two of us. She saw that I was about to cry and handed me a tissue.

"Sit down, honey, I want to talk to you." I sat, fearful of what was going to happen. In a gentle voice, she continued. "Faye, I know it's hard having such a difficult dad. But what he does, whatever he does, is not your fault. And just because he's like he is doesn't mean that you're going to be like him. Not at all. You're your own person, and you can choose how you want to be. You get to decide. Don't forget that, all right?"

I nodded, unable to speak.

She said, "Now please get Francie. We're ready to leave to see the Christmas lights."

Valencia was known for its display of Christmas lights. I hadn't seen them yet and was so excited I had a hard time sitting still as Francie's dad drove us into town and parked. Kyle had gone over to his girlfriend's house, so it was just the four of us. The town square had been transformed into fairyland—thousands of blinking lights adorned all the trees, the bushes, and buildings. I didn't care that most of the trees were palms. They looked beautiful. The town had even trucked in a little snow so kids could throw snowballs at each other. I walked around, transfixed by the magic of the evening.

The cold had settled in, with the temperature hovering around freezing. If you haven't experienced that level of Florida cold, you won't understand. But it seemed colder even than in Ohio. My new jacket was perfect. I zipped it up and felt warm and toasty.

We walked around the square, marveling at the lights. Three quarters of the way around, Francie's dad yelled, "Nisay! Over here." He glanced at Francie and me and explained. "That's the Cambodian man and his family we've been helping get settled. Laney and I took them some things this morning. Come say hello."

Walking toward us were a small man and woman, and four children ranging in sizes from around my age to first-graders, all holding hands. Every one of them had a look on their faces like they were afraid they were going to be kicked, and they seemed to cower under our attention.

The oldest boy looked to be about my age. He was my height and skinny. He probably weighed even less than I did. I might have seen him at school, but he flitted around the edges of the classrooms like he was always in hiding. Tonight, he appeared to be wearing three or four shirts of different sizes, but even so, I could see that he was shivering.

Nisay introduced his wife and children to us. I could barely understand his strongly accented English, but I nodded politely. He grabbed Francie's dad's hand and pumped it. "Thank you, Mr. Ivey, for the food you brought. We had nice meal. And thank you for the clothes. They are very helpful."

I could hardly breathe. I had taken this jacket, even though I had a winter coat, merely because I wanted it. I didn't really need it, despite the fact that I had convinced myself I did. But this boy, whatever his name was, needed it for real.

I thought about Francie's mom telling me I could make my own choices, and I realized, if I were going to be different from my dad, I needed to make a different choice than the one I had made earlier in the day. The world wasn't all about me and my ideas of what I needed to feel accepted.

Understanding what had to be done, I rubbed my hand one more time down the sleeve of the jacket I loved. I knew I would remember the feel of the soft cloth on my skin for a long time. Then I slowly unzipped the jacket, pulled it off, and handed it to the boy. He gave me a questioning look. I gestured that it was his and he should put it on. He did. A smile filled his face. That coat must have been warm from my body heat as well as from its padding.

Nobody spoke for what seemed like a long while. Finally, the boy's dad said, "Thank you, little miss." They all bowed a little and moved on. "Happy Christmas," he called over his shoulder.

"That was nice of you, Faye," said Laney. "But now we should get you home before you freeze to death." Francie squeezed my hand but said nothing. We turned toward the car.

Strangely, I didn't feel the least bit cold as I walked to the car. I had made my own choice. I wasn't my dad. And I understood how great Santa probably felt when he handed out gifts.

Other things happened in the next few months that would change my life. But that's another story I'll save for another time. I just want you to know that that Christmas was the most magical one I can ever remember. I never regretted giving up that jacket.

It was just a jacket, after all.

BOOKS BY DIANE

Who She Is
(https://www.dianebyington.com/who-she-is/)

The Second Time Traveler
coming soon from Red Adept Publishing

ANTHOLOGIES INCLUDED IN

166 Palms (2018)

166 Palms (2017)

Nature's Healing Spirit

American Fiction Vol. 14

ABOUT DIANE

Diane Byington is the author of the award-winning novel, *Who She Is*. Diane has been a tenured college professor, yoga teacher, psychotherapist, and executive coach. Also, she raised goats for fiber and once took a job cooking hot dogs for a NASCAR event. She still enjoys spinning and weaving, but she hasn't eaten a hot dog or watched a car race since.

Besides reading and writing, Diane loves to hike, kayak, and photograph sunsets. She and her husband divide their time between Boulder, Colorado, and the small Central Florida town they discovered while doing research for her novel.

GET IN TOUCH

Diane Byington website: www.dianebyington.com
Facebook author page: https://www.facebook.com/dianebyingtonauthor/
Twitter: https://twitter.com/dianebyington
Instagram: https://www.instagram.com/dianebbyington/
Goodreads: https://www.goodreads.com/book/show/38084780-who-she-is

A Muse-ing Christmas
Ms. Parker Teaches Santa—Shakespeare Style

BY KELLEY KAYE

Leslie Parker teaches high school English (and this year Science Fiction!) at Thomas Jefferson High School in Pinewood, Colorado. She is sassy and snarky with a good, gold heart stuffed in her Louboutin stilettos. She is best friends with a newer teacher, Emma, whom she considers her protegee. She is obsessed with Shakespeare, quoting him as commentary for any situation. Over the past few years, she's been quoting more from the tragedies, because between classes, she and Emma have had to solve murders. For the holiday, the focus is not on murder, but sonnets. And teaching.

This Chimney's Getting Too Damn Tight
a poem

by Maisie Duchovny—
no relation to that X-files actor, David.
I wish!

I remember back in the day.
I'd slide down like a greased hog,
and land lightly like a fog
       that sits on a swamp.

No more.

It takes an ugh
and a tug of those paunchy regions
squirming and writhing,
twitching and wriggling,
and
       oh crap—did I just tear my coat?

When were these logs here before?

They fly out from under my feet
like those barrels
that circus people walk over,
only I can't stay on.

Too fat.

At least they're not on fire, like at the Anderson's house.
What are people thinking, anyway?
Cookies, milk, and spontaneous combustion?
A caloric, lactose-intolerant coal-walker.
Maybe a little bit like Ghandi
plus a few hundred pounds.

Oof, I'm in.

Checking my list–Ms. Lovett, Ms. Parker, Mr. Wells, even Mr. Dixon.

Damn.

No good kids here anyway.

Maisie's poem is delightful, but I wanted her to experiment more along the lines of creativity within constraints, so we learned the two formats for a sonnet: Petrarchan 14 lines 10 syllables per line, iambic pentameter with an abbaabba cdecde octet/sestet rhyme scheme, or Shakespearean abab cdcd efef gg four quatrains and a heroic couplet rhyme scheme. Since her poem naturally ended with a solution to Santa's problem (plus, she just liked that it's called HEROIC), we went with the Shakespearean format. Oh, and it was invented by Shakespeare, AmIRight? Of course I am.

Lamentings from the Smokestack Space
A sonnet of the Shakespearean form

by Ms. Parker and Maisie

On reminiscent, trembling years of youth-
I'd navigate with ease the chimney's neck.
But now I'm forced to reckon with the truth.
My girth is too expansive: What The Heck?!

My wriggle down the op'ning seems a trick
Performed by slender, almost wraithlike types.
The logs to build the fire now prove slick,
For beings of a more athletic stripe.

Much struggling for purchase tears my coat
Frustration levels mounting to a peak
A growling, snarling anger fills my throat
There aren't even cookies here to sneak!

On noticing this list of girls and boys
No single one deserving of my toys!

Whew.

*(Maisie argued with me about the extra syllable at the end, but I claimed
poetic license. Plus, I'm the teacher. "From his cradle/He was a scholar,
and a ripe and good one/Exceeding wise, fair-spoken, and persuading."
Henry VIII. Yeah.)*

BOOKS BY KELLEY

Death by Diploma,
Book 1 in the Chalkboard Outlines Cozy Mystery Series,
written under the pseudonym Kelley Kaye.
https://www.goodreads.com/book/show/26809659-death-by-diploma

Poison by Punctuation,
Book 2 in the Chalkboard Outlnes Cozy Mystery Series,
written under the pseudonym Kelley Kaye.
https://www.goodreads.com/book/show/39694071-poison-by-punctuation/

Down in the Belly of the Whale,
a Young Adult Paranormal Novel,
written under the pseudonym Kelley Kay Bowles.,
https://www.goodreads.com/book/show/36540511-down-in-the-belly-of-the-
whale

ABOUT KELLEY

Kelley (Kelley Kaye, Kelley Kay Bowles, Kelley Gusich) taught High School English and Drama for twenty years in Colorado and California, but her love for storytelling dates back to creating captions for her high school yearbook. Maybe back to the tales she created around her Barbie and Ken.

A 1994 MS diagnosis has (circuitously) brought Kelley, finally, to the life of writer and mother, both of which she adores. *Death by Diploma*, released by Red Adept Publishing in February 2016 and #1 for cozy mystery on Amazon in August that same year, is her debut cozy mystery, first in the Chalkboard Outlines® series. Book 2, *Poison by Punctuation,* was released April 24, 2018. Her debut Young Adult Paranormal, *Down in the Belly of the Whale*, received the 2017 Indie Book of the Year from Aionios Books, who published the book May 5, 2018.

GET IN TOUCH

Kelkay1202@yahoo.com
https://www.kelleykaybowles.com
https://www.facebook.com/authorkelleykaye/
https://www.bookbub.com/authors/kelley-kaye
https://www.goodreads.com/author/dashboard
https://www.youtube.com/channel/UCVlte3qfP3gTpHOwjNjqDqg/
https://www.youtube.com/watch?v=3-Is8SGcAWg

Building Cairns

BY DARREN LEO

She sat on the porch, in an Adirondack chair made from sawed up skis, and watched sparrows dance on the edge of a bird bath. They splashed then shook and created tiny, instant rainbows. Her long braid, a loose mess of grey hair, hung down one side of her neck. The young people said she looked like Katniss, but she didn't know who the hell that was.

A group of hikers were at the picnic table under the big elm and drinking beer. They were young and, almost halfway through their hike, very fit and brash. She didn't mind the through hiker bros. After twelve hundred miles of walking, they had earned some bravado. She preferred the other hikers that wandered into their little outfitter shop and hostel, and one was trudging up the road now.

At first she thought he was old because of the silver hair. As he neared, she saw that he was perhaps in his early forties. His pack and boots were top quality and not very old. She could see from his slumping shoulders that the pack was poorly fitted and carried way too much.

"Is this the hostel?" he asked with the wheezing voice of someone over exerting and under hydrating.

"Honey, if you can't tell that it is, I ought to make you hike right back to the woods," she said.

"So that's a yes?"

She studied him. In a life a long time ago, she held a doctorate of psychology. It came in handy in her official duties as hostel keeper and unofficial duties as tribe mother. There were many types of hikers who wandered into her home. The gap years, bucket listers and experience junkies were the most common. The spiritual pilgrims annoyed the shit out of her. The refugees always had the most interesting stories.

"Drop your pack and pull up a chair."

He actually dropped the pack where he stood and collapsed into a chair. It was a beautiful, cool day, and Indian summer was lingering even as Christmas came around the bend, but he had sweated completely through his clothes.

"I'm Frog. Welcome," she said.

"Atlas," he replied and gulped from his water bottle.

Anyone who spent enough time on the trail adopted, or was given, a trail name. She was intrigued by his.

"Holding up the weight of the world?" she asked.

"As in Titan. I obviously don't know much about Greek mythology." He said it with a smile but no joy.

"Where'd you start?" she asked.

"Harper's Ferry."

That was about a hundred pretty easy trail miles south. A fit hiker would do it in four or five days.

"How long you been out?" she asked.

"Two weeks."

She had seen the midlife escapees plodding into a world they were not prepared for, but they had determination and a desire for adventure. All she saw in him was resignation. She thought again that the refugees had the most interesting stories.

"So, you're NoBo?" she asked.

He looked at her blankly and drank more water.

"Northbound, as opposed to SoBo, southbound."

"Sure."

They watched golden leaves fluttering until he stopped gasping, and she showed him around, where to pitch his tent, the outdoor shower, and the washing machine.

"Sometimes I cook and share. Sometimes I don't. Don't ask me. I'll tell you." This was part of her routine, but he didn't strike her as one who would come with entitlement.

"Thank you," he said and began setting up his camp, and she watched. He was efficient. Everything went in its place. He was not one who would discover he left his water purifier nine miles back.

That evening, after the pffft of camp stoves being shut off and the quick inhalation of food that all distance hikers practiced, the group sat on her porch.

Frog sat down by Atlas who was a little away from the main group. The alpha hikers discussed the distance they'd cover the next day and when they were starting.

"Hey Atlas. You're a section hiker right?" One asked. Frog knew it was an insult more than a question. Section hikers did some portion of the trail as opposed to its entirety.

"Yes," he replied without looking up.

"So are you," Frog said and looked over her glasses at the young man.

"I'm a through hiker, MEGA," he replied. His hiker beard was carefully trimmed and cleaned and Frog hadn't liked him as soon as he arrived.

"Until you stand on Katahdin and Springer, you're not a through hiker," she replied, and that sent the young bucks to bed.

Frog and Atlas watched fireflies skip about on the edge of the irrigation ditch. The breeze carried notes of a fire somewhere. She enjoyed how long the autumn lingered in her little nook of the world.

"What's MEGA?" Atlas asked.

"Maine to Georgia. GAME is Georgia to Maine, or NoBo. You should probably learn these terms."

He shrugged, but she caught a hint of an actual smile in the lantern light.

The next morning she felt slightly bad for putting the bucks in their place so she made blueberry pancakes and bacon. They devoured it like starved wolves. There was a reason that there were no all you can eat buffets near the Appalachian trail. They were long up the trail before Atlas wandered onto her porch.

"You missed breakfast," she called from a flower bed where she was on her knees in the dirt yanking weeds.

"I'm sorry."

"I saved you some bacon and pancakes in the kitchen. Probably need to be microwaved."

He returned some time later with a hint of blueberry on his lips, kneeled in the dirt near her, and began pulling weeds.

"Thank you for the breakfast."

"You don't have to pull weeds to be fed."

"I kind of enjoy it. If you don't mind. Reminds me of being a boy."

They clawed at the dirt, and the cool sun reached up behind them. He told her of spending summers in upstate New York, at his grandparents' orchard, working in the earth and dirt.

"Is it okay if I spend another night here?" he asked.

"Taking a zero?" she asked. He stared at her.

"A zero is a zero mileage day. No hiking."

They continued to grab and pull at the invasive plants, and she was carefully plucking weeds from a stack of rocks.

"It's a cairn," she said before he asked.

"A what?"

"Have you ever hiked or backpacked?"

"Before I spent my first night on the trail, no."

She explained that cairns were stacks of rocks used to mark a trail above treeline or in deserts. They were symbolic of finding one's way. Hers was perhaps two feet tall, made up of rounded river rocks.

"When," she paused, "if, you make it to the White mountains you'll see cairns."

"Why do you have this one?"

"It's a memorial." She didn't expound, and he didn't ask.

He helped her drag kayaks to the barn, nail a loose shutter, and clean out the hiker shower. Three Miles always cautioned her about taking in strays, as he called it, but he did it too, and her husband was off hiking for a month. That thought reminded her that he'd be home soon with a bunch of the tribe in tow for the holidays. She'd have to get to baking and decorating.

A new batch of hikers began to arrive in the afternoon. Frog and Atlas sat on the porch, and she described each hiker as they neared. Two women were a mother and daughter. The father had recently passed away, and they were spending a week on the trail to commemorate him. An early twenties hiker with thick framed glasses had just graduated college and was doing the AT before beginning grad school. She continued on. In conversations later with the hikers, Atlas found her to be highly accurate.

Later, making her rounds to ensure each hiker was settled in, she found him in front of his tent looking at photos.

"May I?" she asked, and he handed her the pictures. All were of Atlas and an attractive woman in her mid to late thirties. They smiled at Niagara falls. She held up the leaning tower of Pisa. Holding hands, they leaped off a pier in Aruba. She held a teacup, with her pinky out, at tea in London. They weren't the sort of pictures to pine over after a break up. They were memorial photos. Put them in a pile, and they'd be a cairn.

"My condolences. It is so hard to lose a loved one." she said as she handed the memories back to him. He wiped a tear away from his cheek.

She sat beside him and dug her flask out of a cargo pocket. She sipped and passed it to him. He took a long pull of the cheap bourbon and sobbed.

"I was a trader on Wall street. I was a good trader. Big apartment on the upper east side, summer place in the Hamptons, traveled all over the world. Master of the universe," he paused and his voice broke, "a titan."

A groundhog waddled near, rising on its hind legs to scan the air for food or predators. Frog listened and looked at the clover around her feet.

"How did she pass?" she asked.

"Cancer. It spread quickly. I took her to Boston. We went to the Mayo clinic. I found the best doctors on the planet, convinced that effort and money could beat it."

He took another drink. She waited. She knew the ending of the story, but he should have the right to tell it.

"Five months later she was dead. Master of the universe." He said it with self-hatred. "Master of nothing."

"And so now you're on the trail seeking refuge." The refugees always had the most interesting stories. By definition, they were never happy ones.

The moon, bloated and full poked over the trees, and the world became black and white and shades of grey.

"Master of nothing."

"That's a shitty trail name. Some find their peace in the trees. Some don't. I hope you find yours." She shrugged. Platitudes provided no benefit so she didn't offer them.

Winter decided to arrive the next morning. The air was cold, and her songbirds squawked their displeasure from the comfort of their nests. Atlas trudged up the road with his pack and the weight of the world on his bowed shoulders. She finished nailing a string of Christmas lights over the porch and went to the garden.

She pulled a smooth, flat oval of a rock from her coat. She'd fished it from the river last summer. She sought out the refugees and their stories. In her mind she liked to think maybe she could absorb some of the weight they carried just by knowing the story. With care and both hands, she balanced the stone on the cairn. Each story killed her just a little.

BOOKS BY DARREN

The Trees Beneath Us

ABOUT DARREN

Darren R. Leo grew up in Utah skiing more than he went to school. He received a BA from the University of Utah in English where the writing bug first bit him. He kept it latent and endured a successful and award winning career in the hotel industry. He returned to school and earned his MFA in Fiction from Southern New Hampshire University in 2013.

His novel, *The Trees Beneath Us* was published by Stark House Press in 2015. His short stories have appeared in *Crack the Spine, The Atticus Review, The Blue Lake Review*, and several other literary journals and anthologies.

Darren served in the army, fell out of airplanes, climbed mountains, raced bicycles, hiked the Appalachian Trail, is a good cook and a bad gardener, and will try almost anything; much to the chagrin of the very patient woman he lives with in Rhode Island.

GET IN TOUCH

Website: www.bootson.com
Facebook: https://www.facebook.com/drleowriter/?ref=bookmarks
Goodreads: https://www.goodreads.com/book/show/25450417-the-trees-beneath-us?from_search=true

A Katie Christmas

Featuring Cooper and Katie from
To Katie With Love

BY ERICA LUCKE DEAN

A light dusting of snow dotted the sky as Cooper pulled into the bank parking lot for the client-appreciation holiday brunch. He counted three other BMWs in the lot besides his—two red and one white, as if they'd color coordinated for the occasion. *Maybe I should wait until after Christmas. Hell, maybe I should wait till after the new year.* What was another week when he'd had a *thing* for his banker for almost a year without acting on it?

With the engine still running, he darted his eyes to the rear view, running a shaky hand through his hair before exhaling into his cupped hand. *Peppermint.* He straightened his red tie for the umpteenth time since putting it on and fastened his top jacket button while contemplating heading back home. "I should've worn the gray suit."

Before he could back out, his *former* banker, the slightly terrifying Silvia *Something*—it was right on the tip of his tongue—burst through the door and rushed toward his idling car. The woman was tiny but formidable. He understood why the entire bank considered her the de facto manager, whether she carried the title or not.

Silvia wagged a manicured finger at him from outside his car window and shook her head. Somehow, her spiky amber mane didn't move a centimeter. Even though he couldn't hear a word she said with the engine running and the heater on full blast, he could read her lips, loud and clear. "Cooper Maxwell, don't you dare chicken out, again!"

"Shit," he muttered. *Caught.* He unbuckled his seatbelt and killed the engine, sending up a silent prayer for strength as he grabbed the wrapped gift from the seat beside him and climbed out. "Yeah, yeah, I know. I'm coming."

"Don't sass me." Silvia snatched the package from his hands, tucking it under her arm as she expelled a cloud of hot breath. "She's leaving right after brunch to spend Christmas with her family, so this is your last chance until next year."

Cooper chuckled. "Silvia, next year is two weeks away."

"No more stalling. You've been secretly in love with her—"

He grunted but couldn't ignore the truth anymore.

"Don't even think about denying it." She narrowed her eyes at him, pursing her rust-colored lips until the lines around them puckered. "You've had a crush on Katie James since the girl started here, and I'm tired of watching the two of you dance around each other like a pair of lovesick teenagers. It's time to act!"

Definitely formidable.

"What makes you so sure she'd even agree to go out with me?" Cooper shoved a hand through his hair then quickly smoothed it down again. He almost felt stupid for being so insecure, but Katie James wasn't just any girl. She was smart, funny, kind, and whether she knew it or not, beautiful.

"Trust me. All she needs is a little push."

"When you say push—"

Before Cooper could finish his sentence, Silvia pulled him into the building and all but dragged him into her office. With a quick scan of the lobby, she shut the door and placed the wrapped package on her desk. "So is this what I think it is?"

"Of course. You said she loved—"

"Love?" Silvia snorted. "That's an understatement. She's absolutely *obsessed* with these books."

With wide eyes, he dropped into the chair across the desk from her and glanced toward Katie's office. "Really?" He wasn't sure if this knowledge worked in his favor... *or not.*

"You have no idea. She'll be utterly thrilled to have the next one in the series. She talks about the vampire character as if he's a real person. I swear she could describe his rakish good looks and dark sense of humor for hours." Silvia rolled her eyes. "As if any man could actually live up to that."

Cooper shifted in his seat and brushed a speck of lint from his perfectly pressed trouser leg. "So basically, I'm competing with a fictional character for her attention?" Did he even have a chance with Katie if her idea of the perfect man was a dark, dangerous vampire? He certainly didn't look the part in his navy bespoke suit, with his hair parted to one side and slicked back like a run-of-the-mill investment banker or corporate lawyer. Hell, even his hands were freshly manicured. *Pussy.*

"Basically." Silvia nodded absently. She didn't seem to notice his discomfort. "I'm almost positive that girl will spend the rest of her natural life with her nose in a book if we don't do something about it."

"That's—"

"Crazy? I know. But that's our Katie."

Cooper caught a glimpse of the object of his desire scrambling across the lobby, with her dark hair swinging frantically over her shoulders and a determined spark in her green eyes. He sighed. He'd sat across from her twice a week for almost a year, and like an idiot, hadn't found the guts to make a move. What would she say if she knew what he did for a living? "I don't think she's crazy. I think she's beautiful…"

"You're as bad as she is."

"I guess that's a good thing, right? But…" Guilt twisted Cooper's insides. "Do I tell her—"

"Your secret? Well, of course. You'll have to… eventually. But we both know she's not ready for that yet. Give her some time to get to know you a little first."

He had to agree. He wasn't ready to come clean just yet either. Silvia knew the truth, of course. Keeping a secret from *her* was near to impossible. The woman had a sixth sense and the instincts of a bloodhound. Even if she hadn't sniffed out the truth, he would've eventually caved.

Silvia slid the package to her side of the desk to inspect his expert wrapping job. He'd even tied the bow with his own two hands. His mother would be proud.

Silvia flicked the tag with a fingernail until Katie's name, scrawled out in elegant script, faced up. "You didn't sign it?"

He shrugged. "I wanted to write something, but I didn't know what to say."

Silvia tossed back her head and let out a loud bark of laughter.

Cooper slumped down in the chair and crossed his arms like a spoiled child. "I'm glad you find that so funny."

"Oh, I really do."

Cooper heaved out a breath. "So what's the plan?"

Silvia's face lit up, and she rubbed her hands together like the evil genius she was. "Mistletoe!"

It didn't take long for the lobby to fill with an assortment of people grazing on mini quiches, fancy pastries, and chocolate-dipped berries. The aroma of freshly brewed coffee and baked goods filled the air. Cooper reached for a goblet brimming with some sort of sparkling juice but didn't dare eat. Nervous excitement twisted his stomach into knots.

The jazz soundtrack from *A Charlie Brown Christmas* played in the background as he scanned the perimeter. He recognized a few people, mostly the other employees. One or two faces looked familiar, but he couldn't find the only one he wanted to see anywhere in the crowd.

"Do you think these mushroom puffs have cheese in them?" An older woman with an impressive silver hair helmet nudged his shoulder. As she swayed from side to side, the string of pearls around her neck dipped down until it nearly landed in the gravy boat.

Mushroom puffs? Cheese? Cooper opened his mouth to respond but never got the chance.

"I adore mushrooms, but I simply *can't* eat cheese. You couldn't possibly imagine the horrible things it does to my digestive tract."

"Edna, why don't you try the vegan spinach quiche instead?" Silvia swooped in, throwing Cooper an eye roll as she steered Edna toward another tray of treats.

That was close. The last thing he wanted was to hear exactly what happened to Edna's digestive tract when she consumed too much cheese. He took a sip of his drink and shuddered.

"Not a fan of the spiced cider?"

Cooper spun around, and there she stood, a tentative smile on her pink lips and a question in her green eyes. "Spiced cider?"

Katie gestured to his goblet. "You made a face."

"Oh…" Understanding dawned on him. "No, it's fine, I…" He shot a quick glance over his shoulder then dropped his voice to a whisper. "Someone named Edna tried to give me a lengthy description of her lactose intolerance."

"No!" Katie covered her mouth to laugh, and her hand trembled slightly. "I wouldn't be able to eat after that either."

Cooper's pulse quickened. *She has no idea what she's doing to me.* "What about you? I didn't see you eating."

"Me?" Her voice climbed an octave as she fiddled with the top button on her blouse. "The last thing I need is another gooey pastry."

"Hmm…" He studied the food table, debating how to respond. If he agreed, she might assume he thought she was fat. If he told her he found her to be perfect, she'd think he was overcompensating. *Classic no-win situation.* "Those little things definitely look dangerous. Let's walk away while we still can."

With a nod, Katie led him toward the center of the room. She drew in a shaky breath and cleared her throat. Her shy smile gutted him. "So, Cooper… doing anything exciting for Christmas?"

"Flying home to see my parents, actually."

"Oh! Me too… well, driving home." She choked back a laugh as if she knew something he didn't.

"What's so funny?" He cocked his head to one side, casually appraising her bright eyes and flushed skin. *God, she's beautiful.*

"Katie!" Her obnoxious redheaded coworker shouted at them from across the room, waving her arms over her head.

Cooper couldn't remember her name, but he knew to stay as far away from that one as humanly possible.

The girl cupped her hands around her mouth. "Could I have a word?"

"Oh, um… sure?" Katie nodded then turned to Cooper with an apology in her eyes. "Can you excuse me for just a minute? I'll be right back."

"I'll be right here… waiting."

Katie giggled, and his skin tingled. She glanced at him over her shoulder as she crossed the lobby.

"What are you doing?" He bristled at the sound of Silvia's annoyed voice. He turned to face her, and she planted her small hands on her narrow hips.

"Making conversation?"

"You're supposed to get her over to the mistletoe." Silvia whisper shouted, hooking her thumb toward the rear of the lobby.

He held up his glass. "I needed a little liquid courage first."

"You certainly won't find it in a glass of non-alcoholic cider!" Her voice cracked as she flailed her arms.

Cooper frowned. "Fine. As soon as she's done talking with her friend."

"Friend? Vicky?" Silvia barked out a laugh. "Oh, that's rich."

"What do you mean?" He hazarded a glance toward Katie and Vicky.

Vicky winked at him.

Note to self: avoid Vicky at all costs.

"Never mind." Silvia waved a hand. "Oh, hell. I need to go get Edna before Phil turns an even darker shade of green. The man has a weak stomach and a gag reflex with a glitchy trigger."

Cooper scanned the room for the mistletoe and spotted a tall, leggy blonde heading his way. He'd seen her at the bank before but never paid much attention. While he could admit she was attractive, her stick figure, platinum hair, and icy blue eyes did nothing for him.

Those icy eyes locked on him like a missile, and her lacquered lips curled up at the corners.

"Shit," he muttered as he searched the crowd for Katie. *Where did she go?*

"Well, hello again. It's Cooper, right? Fancy seeing you here." The blonde reached a delicate hand toward him, and Cooper fumbled in his pocket for his phone, pulling it out and quickly pressing it to his ear.

He held up one finger and forced a smile. "Sorry, I need to take this."

Her face fell, but she put on a fake smile and nodded. "Of course. I'll catch up to you after."

Not if I can help it.

As soon as he ditched his tail in the crowd, Cooper pocketed his phone. The Christmas jazz playing from speakers in the ceiling droned on as he circulated among a throng of people he would've typically avoided at all costs; the rich elite with nothing better to do on a Friday morning than stuff their surgically altered faces with microwaved canapés in a bank lobby. *A cocktail party without the cocktails.*

Why am I here? As if to answer his question, Katie's natural, unaffected laugher floated through the room, drawing his attention from talk of business mergers, interest rates, and lactose intolerance. She was the reason for all of it.

After placing his nearly full goblet on a nearby table, Cooper made his way through the crowd to where Katie stood, talking with an exuberant client.

Cooper tapped her on the shoulder. *Call her Katie.* His insides clenched. He couldn't do it. Her friends called her Katie, and until he could break out of the client-zone he'd stick to formality. "Excuse me, Kate. Can I steal you for a second?"

"No, Katie, don't leave!" The other man gripped Katie's hand in both of his and dropped to a knee.

What the hell? A red-hot flare of emotion struck Cooper squarely in the gut.

"Knock it off, Dean." Katie laughed as she tugged her hand free. "Don't mind him; he's being dramatic."

Dean sighed. "You never take my proposals seriously."

"Because they *never* are."

"One day, I'll surprise you."

"I doubt it." She shook her head then turned to Cooper. "I'm sorry, I was on my way back when I ran into Dean."

"So I see." The hair on the back of his neck prickled, and Cooper struggled to keep the smile on his lips while fighting back the urge to strangle Dean where he stood. "He's one of your clients?"

Katie leaned in to whisper. "One of my more colorful clients, yes. He's a little loud and obnoxious but totally harmless."

"Good to know." Cooper glanced over his shoulder to where Dean watched them walk away. *Harmless, my ass.* Cooper recognized the familiar look in Dean's eyes as he watched Katie retreat.

"So where were we?" Katie smiled up at him. Her attention seemed to zero in on the ball of mistletoe hanging just a few feet above their heads.

"Actually…" Cooper cleared his throat. "There's something I wanted to ask—"

"There you are! I was wondering what happened to you." The icy blonde from before zoomed forward, knocking Katie out of her way to get to him.

What the hell?

"I see you found the mistletoe. I guess we have no choice." Without another word, she lunged at him, attaching her glossy red lips to his open, protesting mouth.

Cooper managed to disengage himself from her tentacles but not before Katie wordlessly disappeared into the crowd. "No, Kate, wait!"

"Oh, no…" The blonde fluttered her fake eyelashes and pouted. "Did I interrupt something?"

"As a matter of fact, yes." Cooper fumed. "You did."

"I'm sorry." Her lizard-like smile called her a liar.

With a growl of frustration, Cooper stormed across the lobby toward Katie's office.

"Cooper Maxwell! Glad to see you made it," Phil, the branch manager stopped him halfway there with a clap to the back. "I hope you're enjoying yourself."

"Yes. At least I was." Cooper fought off the urge to flip him off and keep walking. "If you'll excuse me, I need to speak with Kate before she leaves."

"Sorry, you just missed her. She must have left her stove on again or something. That girl took off as if her hair was on fire!"

"Damn it!" Cooper's heart sank, and he shoved a hand into his hair, squeezing until his roots screamed for mercy. "That's just my luck, isn't it?"

"If there's something you need, I can get one of the other bankers to assist you."

"No. I'm fine." Cooper pressed out a stiff smile. "It'll keep."

"All right then." Phil gave him one last light clap on the back. "Well, Merry Christmas!"

"Thank you. Merry Christmas to you, too."

"What happened?" Silvia charged toward him like a bull in Pamplona. "Did I just see Katie's car screeching out of the parking lot?"

"She… we… and then this woman just *kissed* me…"

"What?" Silvia craned her neck to search the room. "What woman?"

Cooper let out a long breath and propped his shoulder against the wall. "It doesn't matter. Kate's gone. I blew it."

"I'll call her." Silvia fumbled for her cell phone. "You can explain."

"No. Don't. I need to rethink this whole thing. I mean, look at me." Cooper motioned to his expensive suit with a groan. He looked exactly like every other stuffed-shirt, rich businessman in the building. "*This* isn't what she wants. She wants dark and dangerous and—" He huffed out a hollow laugh. "Isn't that ironic?"

"Hmmm… Maybe you're right. Maybe you've been going about this all wrong."

"Hey!" His mouth dropped open. "You're supposed to be helping me!"

Silvia laughed. "I am helping you. But first, you need to stop selling yourself short. You may not appear to be her fantasy man on the surface, but I have a feeling you'd give that vampire a run for his money any day of the week. In fact…" She tapped her bottom lip with a fingernail, and her eyes sparkled with mischief. "I think it's time we regrouped. We need to try again after Christmas. And I know *just* the thing."

"I'm almost afraid to ask." Cooper let out a nervous laugh. "But at this point, I'll do anything to get her to notice me."

"You leave everything to me. I have a feeling about you two, and trust me, my instincts are rarely wrong."

"I do trust you—maybe more than I've trusted anyone else in a long time." Giddy anticipation swirled around his gut. "What's the plan this time?"

Silvia grinned from ear to ear. "If Katie James wants a dark, mysterious suitor, we'll give her a dark, mysterious suitor. And honey…" Silvia eyed him top to bottom. "You're gonna knock that girl's socks off!"

BOOKS BY ERICA

To Katie With Love
https://www.goodreads.com/book/show/17737985-to-katie-with-love

For the Love of Katie
https://www.goodreads.com/book/show/33844503-for-the-love-of-katie

Suddenly Sorceress
https://www.goodreads.com/book/show/18757037-suddenly-sorceress

Suddenly Spellbound
https://www.goodreads.com/book/show/27861558-suddenly-spellbound

Splintered Souls
https://www.goodreads.com/book/show/25873786-splintered-souls

Scattered Souls
https://www.goodreads.com/book/show/32699788-scattered-souls

Ashes of Life
https://www.goodreads.com/book/show/24700476-ashes-of-life

Craving Caine
https://www.goodreads.com/book/show/22037743-craving-caine

ABOUT ERICA

After walking away from her career as a business banker to pursue writing full-time, Erica moved from the hustle and bustle of the big city to a small tourist town in the North Georgia Mountains where she lives in a 90-year-old haunted farmhouse with her workaholic husband, her 180lb lap dog, and at least one ghost.

When she's not busy writing or tending to her collection of crazy chickens, diabolical ducks, and a quintet of piglets, hell bent on having her for dinner, she's either reading bad fan fiction or singing karaoke in the local pub. Much like the characters in her books, Erica is a magnet for disaster, and has been known to trip on air while walking across flat surfaces.

How she's managed to survive this long is one of life's great mysteries.

Erica is represented by Kelly Peterson of Corvisiero Literary Agency in New York.

GET IN TOUCH

https://ericaluckedean.com
https://www.facebook.com/ericaluckedean
https://www.twitter.com/ericaluckedean

CONVERGENCE

BY STACEY ROBERTS

got my first Christmas miracle in 1978, when I was seven years old. I found out that the first day of Hanukkah fell on Christmas Eve. We Jews had prayed to our vengeful, desert-dwelling Old Testament God for this very thing.

Convergence.

For every glorious holiday non-Jews had, we had a less-thrilling, watered-down one. The drunken revelry of New Year's matched up with our Rosh Hashanah, where we spent what felt like a year in temple. Christians gave up something for Lent and had their slates cleaned. We did guilt and shame on Yom Kippur, where we cast our sins upon the water and spent another long, boring day at prayer. Easter was a gluttonous riot of candy and ducks and bunnies that somehow celebrated resurrection.

We had Passover in the spring, a feast of flat crackers, bitter herbs, and salt water that somehow celebrated our freedom from the lash of Egyptian slavery. Passover was my mother's favorite holiday—no gifts to give, reminders that our chores paled in comparison to building pyramids in the sand for free, and her usual bad cooking was good by Biblical standards. Her favorite bitter herb was the red onion. It went in everything, overpowering salads, sandwiches, soups, and stews. Her Classic Crunchy Egg Salad was equal parts eggs, eggshells, and red onions.

It tasted like the hollow misery you feel when you realize your servitude will never end.

Easter would have been way more fun.

It had come to pass. The first day of Hanukkah was December 24th. I wouldn't have to play with new toys, wearing new sneakers, unnoticed until Boxing Day, when my friends came out to play with all their new stuff, and expected me to be delighted.

"What do you think of my new bike?" my neighbor Jimmy the Fourth asked. "Christmas present."

"Nice," I said, to be nice. "How do you like my new Erector set?"

"Is that new? Seems like you've always had it."

I had gotten it the day after Thanksgiving. Which was better than what I had gotten the day before – overdone turkey legs, dry stuffing jammed full of red onions, and can-shaped cranberry jelly.

It tasted like the first hard winter in a new land.

I gave my mother a significant Hanukkah list that year. Everything would be on sale because Christmas was imminent. In prior years, when no sales were going on, the gifts were paltry. When Hanukkah fell on November 28th there was no race car set or Star Trek action figures. They were way too expensive. But when the Christmas sales hit, they were dirt cheap.

"How about getting it for me now?" I asked two days before Christmas.

"SSSSSSStace, it's not Hanukkah anymore. Wait till next year. What is *wrong* with you?"

What was wrong with me was that next year Hanukkah was probably going to be the day after Halloween, where the only thing on sale was candy. My mother would never buy candy, cheap or otherwise. Sugar, she said, was bad for our pancreases. Whatever those were.

I held out hope for the race car set in 1978. I ran out and got the paper every morning to check the sales at Toys R Us. I wanted the Aurora AFX Championship Raceway Race Set: twenty-one foot track, two Magna Traction cars with Magnatronic sound, two radio car controllers, pit area, track supports, grandstand, and guardrails. I made daily arguments in favor of it that I was sure would bring my mother over to my side.

"It's perfectly safe, Ma. There are guardrails."

"SSSSSStace. What does it need guardrails for?"

"To protect the fans in the stands."

"Do you have fans to put in the stands?"

I flipped to page two of the Toys R Us Christmas circular. "If you got me the Star Trek and Planet of the Apes action figures I would. Just picture it, Ma. Dr. Cornelius and Mr. Spock, talking centrifugal force from behind the guardrails, safe from decapitation by flying automotive debris. It's very responsible."

She had tuned me out by then, because my father called. They had divorced three years earlier. My mother never gave reasons for her decisions, or at least never the same ones twice. When I asked why my parents got divorced, sometimes it was because he wasn't Jewish, or because he gambled, or because he never wore matching socks. Likewise, when I asked her why she gave me a girl's name instead of a boy's, it was because Stacey was the name of the nurse who took care of her during delivery, or because she named me for her favorite aunt, or because she thought I was going to die. Her only consistency was in handing out nicknames to people. Those never changed—she dispensed titles like a medieval potentate trying to shore up support for her regime, and once you got yours, you were stuck with it for life. My dad's nickname was *son of a bitch*. I listened to my mother's side of the conversation.

"Fred. What do you want?"

"Oh. Is that so? You can talk to the younger one if you want. He's standing right here with the paper, tryin' to get me to buy him a race car set for Hanukkah."

"I don't know why he wants it. He's preoccupied with guardrails."

"He definitely takes after *you*, Fred. No one on my side of the family is odd. I told you we should have him tested. You're such a son of a bitch."

"It's a race track. With cars. I don't know. You ask him."

She shoved the phone at me. Before my dad could get a word in edgewise, I ran through the specifications and virtues of the Aurora AFX Championship Raceway Race Set, with fans in the grandstands from faraway planets.

"That sounds real good, son."

"Tell that son of a bitch that if he paid the goddamned child support, I'd have more money to buy presents with!" my mother shouted.

"Dad, Mom says that if you paid the goddamned child support—"

"I heard her, son."

I was out of reasoned arguments by December 23rd. There was no way the woman couldn't see the advantages of the Aurora AFX Championship Raceway Race Set. The cars had Magnatronic sound, for God's sake. So I just made sure the toy sale section of the paper was face up when I brought it in from the curb.

"You're folding the paper wrong. I like to read the horoscopes first."

My mother was a firm believer in the zodiac signs.

My father was a Sagittarius. "You know what's wrong with your father, that son of a bitch?"

"He doesn't pay the goddamned child support?"

"He's a Sag (pronounced Saj). Always making promises, always letting you down. I should have married an Aries. Leos are very compatible with Aries."

My mother married an Aries in 1980 – Ted the Drug Dealer. He had many positive traits of an Aries – determined, confident, enthusiastic. He was sure that moving our whole family into a used Winnebago for five years while we traveled the country would be a great experience for us all. On the Arian flip side, he was also impatient, moody, short-tempered, and impulsive, like the time he thought it would be a good idea to drive from Florida to Kentucky and harvest impounded marijuana from a field guarded by policemen and Dobermans.

"Ma, as you may or may not know, the Aurora AFX Championship Raceway Race Set has an actual pit area. Very educational."

"You shouldn't work on cars. Your grandfather was killed by a car."

Technically, he was killed by a tractor that flipped over on him. He was unable to jump off because of a gangrenous leg wound.

"Wasn't it gangrene that killed him?"

"SSSStace. His chest was crushed by a tractor. He was dead right away. Gangrene takes forever to kill you."

"But I thought—"

"Capricorns are really such know-it-alls."

I was a Capricorn. I left her to her horoscopes, and the irresistible press of astrological destiny.

We lit the first candle of the Menorah. My brother—Layne the Favorite, two years older than me—did it. I could not be trusted with fire. My mother said it was because I lacked focus, but she was wildly off-base. I was staring at the pile of presents she had kept under the stairs with an unbreakable intensity. There were some wrapped packages that were the right size to be the Aurora AFX Championship Raceway Race Set. I remained hopeful—the holidays were supposed to be all about miracles.

"Which one do we get first?" I asked. My mother handed us two boxes of equal size, only slightly bigger than our hands, wrapped in blue and silver paper with Jewish stars on it. Maybe they were Magna Cars, with Magnatronic sound, one for each of us so we could play together.

I opened mine. Inside were two yellow mesh bags filled with what looked like gold coins. I groaned.

"What?" my mother asked.

They were chocolate coins, made in Israel. You had to peel the gold foil off to expose the dry, unsweet chocolate underneath.

They tasted like having to conquer your new homeland a mile at a time.

"I love these!" Layne the Favorite said.

I handed mine to him and walked out the door.

I sat on the outside steps, shivering. Our neighbor's houses were all lit up—red, gold, and silver. I saw Christmas trees in the windows. Snow had been falling most of the day, and the world was insulated and silent. We still had seven days to go, because once upon a time, the menorah oil that was only supposed to last one night lasted eight. Hanukkah was about conservation. Christmas was about celebratory over-indulgence. I looked over at Jimmy the Fourth's house, lit up like a Yuletide cruise ship, and wished for the optimism of a Scorpio. I had given my mother a list of things I wanted, just like the Goyisher kids annually sent to Santa Claus. The Christians had it made; their methods always worked, but my mother was no jolly order-taker.

The silence was broken by the sound of a car coming up the driveway. I didn't recognize it, but I knew it was my dad. He showed up every year sometime between Christmas Eve and Boxing Day, but we never knew when to expect him. If he had nothing to do around the holidays, it was Christmas Eve. If he was busy, Layne and I often spent Christmas Day waiting in our pajamas, our eyes swiveling between the nearly-muted TV to the front door. We were like kids waiting for Santa Claus. One year I even thought to bait him like my friends did, but instead of leaving out milk and cookies, I was going to put out the only things I ever saw my dad consume: coffee and cigarettes. My mother stopped me when I asked her for two packs of Marlboros and how to work the coffee maker.

My father got out and opened the trunk. I recognized him by his prematurely silver hair and the bright button down shirts he liked. I ran over to him and grabbed him from behind in a deathgrip of a hug. He smelled like Old Spice and cigarette smoke.

"Hey there, son," he said. "I didn't see you." He turned around and knelt down in front of me.

"Did your mother send you outside without a coat?"

"I sent myself out," I said.

"Chocolate coins?" he asked. I nodded. He chuckled. "I never liked them either."

In that moment it occurred to me for the first time that I had more in common with the parent who didn't live at home. This did not bode well.

He lifted two big wrapped packages from the trunk.

"Are those for US?"

He grinned. "Yes. Five pounds of chocolate coins."

"That's not even close to funny."

"Close the trunk for me. Watch your fingers."

I went in first and let him come through with the packages. My brother looked up, his face covered in Israeli chocolate.

"Mother," he said. "Dad's here."

My mother looked him up and down. "You coulda *cawled* first."

"I did call first. You put me on the phone with Stacey."

"Son of a bitch. What do you want?"

"I got Christmas presents for the boys."

My mother's eyes widened. My dad always brought presents over for us at Christmas. My mother said that it was because he only cared about his holidays. I thought it was because he could never figure out what day Hanukkah was. No wonder our towns kept getting sacked by Cossacks. We really needed to get our act together as a people.

Whenever he brought us Christmas gifts my mother would give him her haughtiest look, as if his horsemen had just burned our village to the ground and peed in our well.

"It's. Not. HANUKKAH," she would hiss.

He put the boxes down on the floor. I lurched toward one. He put a hand up without a word and I froze in place.

"Fred," my mother hissed. "It's not Hanuk—"

"Yes it IS!" I howled. "It IS Hanukkah! AND Christmas! Thank you, Jesus!"
My mother glared at me as if I'd asked for a ham sandwich.
"SSSSSStace!"
"Can I open mine? Can I?"
My mother flapped her hands. "Go ahead."
"Go ahead," my dad said.
"You're a real son of bitch, Fred. You know that?"
"Yes," my dad said. "Yes I do."
"Sssso. I guess this means I'm not getting the goddamned child support."
That whole conversation took place over my head. I didn't realize it then, but my father had two voices—the deep, measured one he used when he talked to my mother, or his bookie. The other, lighter, singsong one he saved for when he spoke to me and my brother. It was his voice I grew into years later—I heard it on a videotape of me talking to one of my daughters, the same light singsong.

But in 1978, the only sound I wanted to hear was the ripping of red and gold wrapping paper with reindeer on it. As I shredded it, I could see the words on the package:

AURORA AFX CHAMPIONSHIP RACEWAY RACE SET

I was silent. I had only ever seen it in black and white. This glossy box was covered in lurid reds and yellows. The track was a deep black with white lines, the cars gleamed blue and orange, and even the guardrails were a safe and comforting gray. Seeing this treasure in living color caused my senses to overload. But not for long.

"You got it," I said wonderingly. "Magnatronic sound and everything. Look, Ma! Guardrails!"
Dad reached down and put his hand on my head. He smiled down at me. "So it's the right one."
I nodded, clutching the box.
"Should we go put it together?"
I ran for the living room. He shrugged at my mother and followed me, hearing her whisper *son of a bitch* as he went. I finally understood her frustration years later, after my own divorce. She spent every day with us, making sure we brushed our teeth and did our homework and stayed clean despite our own best efforts. We resented her for it. Our father, who showed up at random, didn't stay long, and never contributed to the household, was treated like a hero. I get it now.

At seven years old, though, I was simply grateful that the miracle of convergence had finally come. It would be another twenty-seven years before

Hanukkah and Christmas ended up on the same night, but I was content to let the future take care of itself.

I had a racetrack to build.

BOOKS BY STACEY

Trailer Trash With a Girl's Name
https://www.goodreads.com/book/show/21481071-trailer-trash-with-a-girl-s-name

Trailer Trash With a Girl's Name: Father Figures
https://www.goodreads.com/book/show/36355995-trailer-trash-with-a-girl-s-name

ABOUT STACEY

Stacey Roberts was born in a smoky hospital in New Jersey in 1971. Nine years later, he and his family moved into a Winnebago and traveled across the country. After several near-death experiences, they settled first in California and then Florida.

He attended college at Florida State University and University of Miami, where he received his B.A. in English Literature instead of Finance, which was a great disappointment to his mother.

He went on to get a Master's degree in Early Modern European History at the University of Cincinnati, to which his mother said, "SSSStace. History? What do you need that for? What is *wrong* with you?"

His mother was right. He didn't need it for anything, except to make arcane references about the Roman Empire or Henry VIII that no one else understands.

He founded a computer consulting firm outside of Cincinnati, Ohio in 1994, and resides in Northern Kentucky with his wife and their two Golden Doodles.

GET IN TOUCH

Facebook: https://www.facebook.com/staceyrobertsauthor/
Twitter: https://twitter.com/sroberts1971

Caesar's Gift

BY LETEISHA NEWTON

The whole deal with fucking Christmas is it's annoying as fuck when you've never bought a damn gift in your life. Okay, that's not completely true. I've just been out of practice. I've spent most of my life destroying everything in my path on my way to the top and enjoying the fruits of my labor as I crushed my enemies into the ground. Hell, I never thought I'd *deserve* more than death served up painfully bloody in a dark alley smelling of shit and bullets.

That's what happens when you're the bogeyman.

Ashlyn changed everything though. She blew into my fucking life to pay a debt—a thing for me to break, control, and *own*—but she fought me every step of the fucking way until I couldn't get enough of her. I caressed the tattoo on the back of my neck in large script. *Precious Ashlyn*. Here I was, the most dangerous man in Florida, in front of a damn department store looking for the perfect gift. Last time I was in a store, I played pretty damn nicely with my Ashlyn for the sales rep to watch. *Score!*

"Hey, C?"

I turned to Collin and lifted one brow. "Yeah?"

"Scared to go in?"

"I'll gut you in your sleep, you know that?"

"Only if I call you by your real name, and I saw what you did to the last guy. It was my job to clean up the mess."

Yeah, that wasn't pretty, but the motherfucker called my wife a bitch while she had my son in her arms. He deserved every bit of crazy I inflicted on him in short order. No one, absolutely no one, disrespected what was mine and what I'd come to love. Tyler was only four months old and didn't understand the words, but he still didn't need that sort of shit in his life. My son would be a monster when the time came, but until then, he'd get the best start in life I never got. To be fair to the redhead who watched my wife and son's backs, he'd beaten his ass to a pulp by the time I arrived and was about to do some real dirty work. Ashlyn seemed to bring out the best in all of us.

"Shut up. I just don't ..." *Uh, no. I'm not going to admit—*

"Know what to get the most amazing woman in your world? Figured."

I clenched my fists. "Keep joking."

Collin shrugged. The big bastard had earned his place in my crew, especially after betrayal from others and more. Ashlyn personally expected him to protect her and my son when they were out; it was how I knew about Bitch Boy and his potty mouth. It was also why I'd brought Collin with me to shop. He knew Ashlyn and Tyler pretty fucking well, better than I sometimes thought I could. Being a mafia don and running shots was a dangerous business that kept me on the move. I didn't get to spend as much time at home as I'd like. And Collin, well, he'd done something very special for Ashlyn when her world was so fucking screwed and I was out of the picture. The shit he did had bonded the two closer than blood. Collin became the brother she should have had instead of that piece of shit I put into the ground for her.

Love—it's a wonderous thing.

"Well," Collin started, rubbing his jaw, "you got rid of her demons, tore Lorcan a new one, got her an education, put her on your skin, gave her a baby, and she's the most feared woman on the East Coast."

I groaned. Fucking shopping was *boring*. This wasn't my sort of fucking story. "Maybe I should just kill someone for her again. She have any other dark skeletons in the closet I somehow missed?"

"C, no one who's ever hurt her is breathing. You made sure of that. And killing someone is *not* a Christmas gift. It's a way to say 'I love you' on random days."

I snorted. "You sure about that? I mean, it could be cool for me to combine it with some sappy Bloody Valentine promise and all that, knock out two holidays in one."

Collin burst out laughing, but I was serious. "No, C. Try again."

"That's why I've got you here."

"And the minute I come up with something better than you, you're going to want me in a pine box for knowing her too well. I'm better off just pointing you in the right direction."

He was … right. I got a bit crazy when it came to my wife and son. I couldn't help it. They'd saved me in ways I never thought possible, and my dark little heart beat just for them. I sighed. Okay, I could do this. But getting something in a department store wasn't going to cut it. Ashlyn could buy anything she ever wanted, and most of the time I was constantly getting her jewelry from the best designers, clothing from the runway, and even handmade toys for Tyler. More *shit* wasn't the way I should go about any of this.

"Okay, change of plans. Gotta think outside the box."

Collin nodded. "I think that'd be best."

I looked at him. I knew Collin's history, the hell he'd gone through before I pulled him out of fighting in underground rings. He'd stood as champion above lesser men, rage boiling through his veins until he couldn't think straight. All that mattered was the next fight, the next opportunity to fuck shit up because he hadn't been able to fight when it really mattered—when he'd needed to protect himself.

"Touchy subject coming, but you know I don't care."

He sighed before motioning to the car. "Can we at least get out of the open for this discussion?"

I nodded, and he escorted me to the sweet-ass Bentley Ashlyn got me for my birthday last year. She'd gone back to school to earn her degree and was probably the highest paid private accountant ever. She worked exclusively for my organization and kept the numbers clean. I slid along the buttery-smooth seats and waited for Collin to close my door before moving behind the driver seat. He pulled off in silence, heading home.

"All right, C. Get it done." His quiet voice filled the cabin, and part of me felt like hell for enjoying the chance to pick at scabs.

Ashlyn had changed a lot about me, but the innate darkness swirling around in my belly would never go away. All the ones around me knew better than to think differently.

"What did you want most after getting away from your mother?"

A muscle worked in Collin's jaw, and I could make out his stern expression from his profile. Fire-red hair left to grow long and restrained into a bun may have looked feminine on other men, but for Collin it added to some deadly cloud around him. It dared a fucker to say some shit just so he could pound faces.

"Freedom," he finally answered.

"Not revenge?"

He shook his head, fingers clenching the steering wheel. "What's revenge when you don't know if you'll even make your own decisions? That your life isn't yours? Revenge comes with freedom and power. I knew how to develop power, it would just take time. But freedom? That shit was priceless."

Collin's mother had been the PTA mom, complete with a football quarterback for a son who was going somewhere. She was perfectly coifed at all times, presentable, and a community activist working with battered children and wives. However, behind the scenes, she pimped out her son to her largest donors. She'd been doing that shit for so many years he thought it was normal and hadn't gotten a taste of freedom until a football scholarship took him to a college clear across the country. Collin never made it to college though. He boarded his plane, disappeared on a layover, and showed up in Europe. I shipped him back to the States after sending him a former abuser's head. I liked fighters, and Collin was one of the best. He wasn't above returning like-for-like treatment when the time came.

"Freedom isn't a tangible thing, Collin."

"No, but it's the answer to your question."

"I gave Ashlyn freedom, remember? She came back to me."

"Oh, you have that confused, C. You gave her a *choice*, and she chose you. You gave her freedom in that warehouse with Trace. You gave her freedom when you helped her hold the knife. You gave her freedom when you got her out of that hellhole with Lorcan. *That* was freedom. Choice is different."

"So what are you saying?"

"I'm saying, freedom is a state of mind long before it is physically felt, if ever. A prisoner can serve time in calm when their mind is free. A man about to die shows no fear because of the same reason. Ashlyn had the strength to come back because you'd already shown her what freedom looked like several times before."

"You know, you irritate the hell out of me when you wax poetic and shit. I like you better when you're turning someone into a meat bag."

"No, you don't."

He was right. I could play the game, the thug, the wild man. All of it was a carefully crafted persona for my enemies to be drawn into. Shit-face crazy, dangerous Caesar St. Clair. They didn't test me because they knew I'd go to any length—and enjoy it. But that didn't mean they were playing with a simpleton to be led around by my rage and dick. Men didn't make it to where I stood on guts alone.

I wouldn't admit that to anyone outside my inner circle though.

"You got me, Collin. The thing is, Ashlyn deserves the world on a platter, and I'd love to give it to her. Or the moon on a golden string tied to her pinky for her to play with. Whatever she wanted, I'd make it happen. If I cou— *Son of a bitch.*"

"What?"

"Franco's about to be pissed, that's what. Get me home, I've got to make a phone call."

"Aren't you mommy's big boy?"

Tyler gurgled as a lopsided grin, so like his father's, transformed his face. I loved this small bundle more than the breath in my body—more than I ever thought possible. His dark ringlets and eyes were Caesar's, but I could see my mouth, nose, and the shape of my chin when I looked at him too. He was a perfect blend of his parents. I kissed his punching fist before rolling him over to rest on his belly. He could fight sleep all he wanted, but it was time for a nap.

Out of habit, my fingertips found the slightly raised ink along my hairline behind my left ear. *Always Caesar.* He bitched about it not being nearly as big as his tattoo of my name, as well as something about me being scared of the pain, and I ignored him as I did all of his jibes. Caesar was a battering ram of emotions and wonderful pain. He knew I could take anything he threw at me. It was why, through all the complaining, I never failed to feel his lips—

Like that.

Warm, soft lips slid up my neck before a sneaking tongue snaked out to trace the tattoo. Shivers raced down my spine as sparks shot off through my bloodstream. Even as his steely arms wrapped around my midsection, I sank against him, soft to hard. Sharp points to concave. We always fit like this: jagged puzzle pieces mashed together and sewn in blood.

"I love you too," I whispered.

"Mmm."

I traced my nails over his forearms. "Use your words."

"Fuck. Now. Love. Hurt."

It was crazy, we both knew it, but those four words were our story. Our way. He'd broken me in so many ways, but he built me up, piece by piece, and in doing so he saved himself.

I spun in his arms. "Your little king isn't asleep yet, and if you mess that up, you won't know where to find your balls before I feed them to you."

His lopsided grin stole my breath. "You know I like it when you talk dirty to me."

"Is the tree up?"

"Yeah."

When he went He-Man on me, there was no way I'd get anything else out of him, so I let my monster take me to bed and hurt me so good.

"Can we finish our conversation now?"

Caesar blinked up at me, his chest rising and falling with each powerful breath. "I didn't do my job well enough if you're up to anything more than sleep."

"Blame it on motherhood. I know the little devil will be up anytime now, ready to eat."

"Well, you're going to have a break soon. I've distracted you long enough."

"What?"

"Get cleaned up and meet me downstairs."

Caesar was out of bed and striding away to the guest room before I even had a chance to ask what the hell he was talking about. Miami sprawled out in front of me through the floor-to-ceiling bulletproof windows of our penthouse master suite in Caesar's condo building. No one but us and members of his organization lived within these walls. It was a haven, a cocoon away from the world. We'd only been attacked once on this turf, and Caesar had upgraded the place to the teeth afterward.

"Kim," I called out, addressing the building's integral virtual assistant.

"Yes, Mrs. St. Clair?"

Damn, I loved hearing that. "Get the shower ready on my settings and rotate closet hangers to dresses."

"Yes, ma'am."

Twenty frantic minutes later, I was wearing a soft, black t-shirt dress that dangled to the floor. I could hear Caesar and Tyler playing together and Collin's rumbling voice as I headed out the bedroom door.

"The queen has arrived," Caesar said.

I froze in my tracks at the top of the staircase. Amidst his men who were standing next to a decorated tree, a line of blood-red rose petals trailed from the stairs and took winding turns around the living room. Statues dotted the room at random stopping points—the Eiffel Tower, the Pyramids, and the Sky Needle in Tokyo.

"What is this?" My voice shook, low and full of awe, but my Caesar heard it. He always did.

Slowly, he looked over at Collin and back to me. "Freedom. Merry Christmas, baby."

"Christmas is a month away, Caesar."

"Yeah, well, we'll be enjoying your gift starting sooner and moving into the new year."

"What?"

"Every place, Ashlyn. Everywhere you ever imagined seeing but never thought you would. The world, baby. Here's the freedom to go wherever you want, whenever you want. Franco will take care of things here, and Collin will come with us to keep an eye on Tyler when we want to be alone."

I nearly stumbled down the stairs, but I made it on shaky feet. My man was there, having already passed Tyler to Collin.

"You've taken me places before, Caesar."

"Not like this. It's your show. It'll always be your show."

"I love you, you know that?"

"Yeah, what else is new." He laughed, but then his eyes grew serious and he cupped my face in his palms. They were hard, rough from violence and strength, but he held me softly. I was precious, *his* precious Ashlyn. "But do you know just how much I love you? I don't think you'll ever understand. I won't die for you, baby. I'll *live* for you. Any way you want me to."

Who was I to argue with the man of my heart?

"Pack the bags," I ordered.

"Already done. We can leave whenever you'd like."

"Now sounds good."

"Now?"

"Now. I'd like to join the Mile-High Club again."

"*Fuck* yeah!"

THE END

Thank you for reading *Caesar's Gift*. I really hope you enjoyed it! Want to see how Caesar and Ashlyn found love? Enjoy Dark Romance? Check out their book here!

http://leteishanewton.com/dark-romance/vanquished

And if you want to come hang out with my reader group, find us here:

https://www.facebook.com/groups/LeTeishaNewtonReader

Or, you can stay up to date on my writings, musings, and learn what #SurvivingWithHades is all about as a member of my newsletter:

http://darkreaders.leteishanewton.com/

BOOKS BY LETEISHA

DARK ROMANCE
THE LOST SERIES

One Hour Girl
Scarred
Phenomenal

STANDALONES

Going Under (MC Dark Romance)
Vanquished (Dark Romance)
Whispers in the Dark (Dark Romance)

MILITARY ROMANCE
A SEALED FATE SERIES

Protecting Butterfly
Protecting Goddess
Protecting Vixen
Protecting Hawk
Protecting Heartbeat

ABOUT LETEISHA

Writing professionally since 2008, LeTeisha Newton's love of romance novels began long before it should have. After spending years sneaking reads from her grandmother's stash, she finally decided to pen her own tales. As many will do during their youth, she bounced from fantasy, urban literature, mainstream, interracial, paranormal, heterosexual, and LGBT works until she finally rested in contemporary romance.

LeTeisha is all about deep angst and angry heroes who take a bit more loving to smooth their rough edges. Love comes in many sizes, shapes, and colors, as well as with—or without—absolute beauty and fairy tale sweetness. She writes the darker tales because life is hard … but love is harder.

GET IN TOUCH

http://leteishanewton.com/
http://facebook.com/AuthorLeTeishaNewton
https://twitter.com/LeTeishaNewton
https://instagram.com/therealleteisha

A Gift for Momma

BY DEBBIE S. TENBRINK

Jo Riskin dug her serving spoon into a tin of steaming scalloped potatoes and dropped a dollop onto the heavy paper plate that Lynae handed her. She held the plate out and met the eyes of the elderly man standing on the other side of the plastic covered table. "Merry Christmas to you, sir."

The old man aimed his piercing blue eyes at her. "A hot meal and people to share it with is all this old man needs to make Christmas merry."

"Then I'm glad we could make that happen. Would you like some help carrying your plate to the table?" she asked, eyeballing the intricately-carved wooden cane he leaned heavily on.

"I can manage," he mumbled as he took the plate in one shaky hand and gripped the cane with the other.

"Of course you can," she said, even as her fingers itched to reach out and steady the plate where the man's dinner quivered and slid dangerously close to the edge.

A little boy who was next in line looked up at the man, his soulful brown eyes peeking out from beneath a Detroit Lions stocking cap. He had come in by himself and hesitantly picked his way through the crowded tables to stand in line. His barely-worn winter coat and fleece-lined boots didn't fit in with the rest of the crowd who gathered for a free meal at Our Daily Bread. He reached up and tapped the old man's arm. "I can help."

The man looked over his shoulder and silently sized the boy up. He stroked his overgrown, gray beard then smiled warmly. "That would be nice."

The boy furrowed his brow and gave a sideways glance to the plate that Jo was taking from Lynae. She dropped potatoes onto the plate and leaned towards the boy. "What's your name?"

"Jerome."

"Don't worry, Jerome, I'll hold onto these for you. Just come right back to me after you help him."

Relief washed over Jerome's face. He took the plate from the old man's hand, then followed him to the table, matching his painfully slow gait. After setting the plate down he hustled to the drink station and brought back two cups of hot cocoa, then walked back to the serving line and waited as Jo filled a plate and handed it to a woman zipped into a sleeping bag with holes cut out for her arms and legs. He took a step back and stared wide-eyed as she walked past him holding an animated conversation with herself.

Jo crooked her finger at the little boy and held up his plate. He smiled shyly and took it from her outstretched hand. "Are you here all alone?" she asked.

The boy's chin dropped to his chest. "Can I still have dinner?"

Jo came around the table and squatted down in front of him. "Of course you can have dinner. I'll even sneak you a little extra if you're still hungry."

Jerome broke into a wide grin. "I really like ham."

"Then you just come right back to me if you want another piece."

"Thank you," he said, then turned and went back to his seat.

Jo kept an eye on him as she served the rest of the people in line. The old man had finished his food and was leaning forward deep in conversation with Jerome. When the last person filtered through the line, she pulled off the thin serving gloves that had melded themselves to her hands, pressed her fingers into her lower back and rolled her shoulders, working out the kinks that had settled in during the almost two-hours she had been standing in the food line. "Well, partner, it looks like the rush is over. I appreciate you spending your Christmas Eve here helping me out."

"There's no place I'd rather be, and I'm not just saying that because you're my Lieutenant and you carry a gun."

"You're a good person. I take back everything I've been saying about you behind your back."

Jo dodged the open palm Lynae swung at the back of her head. "Oh, sure, you start the smack talk now that the rush is over."

"I'm no dummy."

"Besides you *did* invite me to spend Christmas with your family. I would do just about anything for your mom's cooking."

"There *will* be apple pie."

"You had me at *dinner*."

"Well I'm glad you can be my date," Jo said looking up at the banner that hung over the dining area: *Merry Christmas from the Grand Rapids Police Department. Sponsored by the Mike Riskin Foundation.* Jo had started the foundation after her husband was killed in the line of duty. Her heart ached at the thought of spending Christmas without him, but he would be proud of what they were doing tonight and that had to be enough. "I'm going to see what we have left in the kitchen. Keep an eye on Jerome, will you? I don't want him to leave alone, but I sure don't want him to leave with anyone else either."

"Got it."

Jo inventoried their supplies, then took every leftover cookie and brownie and put them on two trays. She slid two cookies and a brownie into a Ziplock bag and set them aside for Jerome to take with him, then pushed through the swinging kitchen door. "Woah!" she exclaimed, executing an impressive pirouette around the cane of the elderly man.

"Excuse me," he said, reaching with his free hand to help her stay on her feet. "I saw you go in there and thought maybe I could talk to you for a minute."

"Sure, what can I do for you?"

"You're a cop, right?"

Jo lifted her chin. "Yes, I am." She looked around him into the dining area, which remained relatively quiet. "Is there a problem?"

"Our little friend, Jerome, he's all alone," he said, glancing over his shoulder.

"I know he is. I'll make sure he gets home safely."

"Thing is, I don't think he's going home."

"What do you mean?"

The man leaned in conspiratorially. "He told me all he wants for Christmas is to make his mom happy and to find a new family to live with."

Jo's stomach clenched. "Did he tell you his last name or where his mom is? Anything else?"

"No, ma'am. I figured you're the police and I would tell you." His brilliant blue eyes twinkled. "I believe he thinks I'm Santa Claus, so I should already know all those things."

Jo took in the man's imposing size, white beard and engaging eyes. Couple that with the unique cane, and to a child he most certainly could be Santa. "Well I'm glad he met Santa while he was here. Thank you for bringing his situation to my attention."

"So you'll take care of him?"

"Yes I will. He'll be safe with me." She turned to survey the dining area teaming with people. Jerome sat safely in his seat, drinking hot cocoa. Some people milled about, but most sat quietly by themselves slowly eating the hearty meal. The few families that had come as a unit huddled in small groups, simulating a private family meal in the public place.

Armed with this new information, Jo's first order of business was to talk it through with her partner. Perhaps the gentleman Jerome had already confided in could get more information out of him. "What's your name, sir?" she asked turning back to the stranger. He was gone. She did a full-circle scan of the room, but he was nowhere to be found.

How did he get out of here so fast?

She took her dessert trays back to the serving line where her crew stood chatting. "Nae, want to help me pass out some to-go desserts?"

"You bet! I love being the hero."

Jo handed her a tray. "We have a problem."

"What, no chocolate chip left?" Lynae said eyeing the trays.

"Even more important than chocolate."

"That's a thing?"

"I'm afraid so. It sounds like Jerome truly is by himself. At least according to the man who was sitting with him."

"Oh, no, poor little guy," Lynae moaned.

"It sounds like he has a family but wants to find a new one. I want to talk to him, but then I'll have to get CPS involved."

"On Christmas?"

Jo shrugged. "What choice do we have?"

"Well, we're detectives."

"We're *homicide* detectives."

"What's the difference?" Lynae asked.

"Oh I don't know, maybe everything. I'm used to a body, forensics, an autopsy, a killer. A victim who isn't still alive."

"Come on, Lieutenant, clues are clues."

Jo sighed. "Let me talk to him and see what I can find out."

Lynae held out her free hand. "Give me your tray. I'll get someone else to help pass these out."

"First call Missing Persons. Maybe there's been a report filed and this will be easy," Jo said as she handed over the tray. She snatched two chocolate chip cookies from it, then headed for the drink station. After getting herself some coffee and another cup of cocoa for Jerome, she eased into the seat across the table from the young boy who sat with his head down. She slid the cocoa and a cookie in front of him. "How was your dinner?"

"Good," he said quietly. He lifted his hands from his lap and laid a photo next to his plate. Keeping one hand protectively on the picture, he reached for the cookie.

Jo glanced at the picture. Jerome and a lovely woman with spiral curls beamed at the camera. Her arm was wrapped protectively around his shoulder, his head tilted to touch the brightly-colored material of her shirt.

"I understand you're looking for a new family."

Jerome peered at her, his brown eyes melting her heart. "He told you?"

"He's worried about you and thought I could help."

"Do you know where I can find one? A new family, I mean."

"I'm a police officer. Why don't you tell me why you need one."

Jerome's eyes grew as wide as tea saucers. "You're a cop? Am I in trouble?"

"No, you're not in trouble. I want to help you. I heard for Christmas you also want to make your mom happy. That's very nice. Are you trying to find your mom? Is that what will make her happy?"

Jerome shook his head. "No, I ran away to make her happy."

Jo's heart sunk. Somewhere there was a frantic mother looking for her son. "Now how would running away make your mom happy?"

"She has too many kids."

"Maybe we should talk to your mom and see if *she* thinks she has too many kids. Can you tell me your last name or your phone number?"

He shrugged and took a bite of his cookie, avoiding eye contact. Jo took a sip of coffee and watched him over the rim of her cup. She had been a detective long enough to know the look. He wanted to tell her, but he was afraid he would get himself in trouble.

Her phone signaled, and she glanced at a text message from Lynae: *Nothing from missing persons.*

"I bet your mom is very worried about you," she said gently.

"She doesn't know I'm gone. She's at work."

"Do you know where your mom works?"

His face scrunched into a picture of concentration. "No, but she's always tired when she comes home."

Jo glanced back at the photo. *That shirt could be a uniform. Scrubs?*

"Were you home alone?"

"No, my sister's there, but she won't even care I'm gone," he mumbled.

"I'm sure that's not true, Jerome."

"She just goes in her room and tells me to leave her alone."

Jo smiled. "That's what big sister's do."

"She's nice to Lainey and Chapman." He stared at the door and took a deep breath. "I have to go."

"Where are you going to go?"

"I don't know."

"It's pretty cold outside." She looked into her empty cup. "I'm going to get some more coffee. Why don't you sit with me a little longer, and have another cup of cocoa before you go."

He nodded, blinking back tears. On her way to get drinks, Jo detoured to where Lynae stood talking to a young couple wrangling a squirming toddler. As she sidled up beside her partner, Lynae turned and grinned. "Speak of the devil. This is Lieutenant Riskin."

The man held out his hand. "Thank you for providing this meal for us. We don't like to take handouts, but we fell on some hard times and this helps."

"As my husband used to say, "It's not a handout, it's making a meal for friends we haven't met yet.""

"Your husband sounds like a good man."

"He was a very good man." She laid a hand on Lynae's forearm. "When you have a minute."

"Right behind you."

After Lynae extricated herself from the young couple, she jostled through the crowd, swinging her now empty tray. Jo poured drinks while keeping an eye on Jerome until her partner joined her. "I need you to make a call for me. I'm afraid if Jerome sees me on the phone I may spook him into bolting."

"Of course, who am I calling?"

"The hospitals. I think we're looking for a nurse in her late thirties, African American, who has four kids. Jerome couldn't have walked that far to get here so she has to live pretty close by."

"How do we know she's a nurse?"

"Jerome has a picture of him and his mom. I didn't get a great look at it, but it appears she's wearing scrubs."

"Okay, now we're getting somewhere," Lynae said pulling her phone from her pocket.

Jo took her time getting back to her seat, keeping an eye on Jerome while stopping to talk to several patrons, giving Lynae as much time as possible to do her investigative work. When Lynae stepped out of the kitchen with a defeated look, Jo's heart sunk.

I'm going to have to call CPS on Christmas Eve.

When Jerome pulled his coat on, she made a beeline for the table. She peered over his shoulder as he picked the photo up from its place next to his empty plate and slid it into an outside pocket of his backpack. Blue mittens dangled on strings from the wrist of his coat.

Her shirt has tiny balloons on it. The hospital nurses wear plain navy.

Jo whipped out her phone and tapped out a message to Lynae: *Try the Children's Hospital.*

Jerome slipped a cookie into his pocket then hoisted his backpack to his shoulder. Jo laid her hand over the little boys trembling fingers. "I'm not going to let you leave alone, Jerome."

"I can't go back. Mom will be happier with one less mouth to feed," he said, wiping away a stray tear that slid down his cheek.

"Why don't you show me what you have in your backpack, so I can be sure you have everything you need."

Jerome regarded her suspiciously then unzipped his bag and pulled out its contents: two shirts, one pair of pants, his teddy bear and a Bible. Jo bit her tongue as tears sprung to her eyes. "Looks like you have everything you need," she said with a serious nod.

Lynae waved a hand and gave Jo the thumbs up, then splayed her fingers. *Ten minutes.*

Relief washed over Jo in a crashing wave.

While Jerome slowly packed his belongings back into his bag, she watched the door. Finally, it swung open and a frantic woman rushed in, her head on a swivel scanning the room. Jo raised a hand, and when the woman's eyes landed on her son she dropped to her knees and burst into tears.

"Does that look like someone who's happy to have her little boy gone?" Jo asked.

"Momma?" Jerome ran to his mom, flung himself into her outstretched arms and buried his face in her neck.

The woman wrapped her arms around her son and rocked back and forth, as tears streamed down her face. She pulled back and looked into his eyes. "Why did you run away?"

"I wanted to make you happy for Christmas."

"Baby, how would losing you make me happy?"

Jerome shrugged. "I heard you tell Granny you have too many kids, and that if you didn't have so many mouths to feed you could get a car and not have to take the bus to work. You could have lots of things that you want."

The woman dropped her head, her curls springing around her face. "I'm so sorry you heard that. Sometimes grown-ups say really dumb things that they don't mean." She took his face in her hands and kissed his forehead. "You and your brother and sisters are the most important thing in the world to me. You are the greatest gifts I could ever have and I thank God every day for you."

"Breslyn would be happy if I was gone. She calls me *little dork.*"

"She'll deny it, but your sister loves you. And I'll be having a talk with her about all this."

"Can we go home now?"

"Well, I'm probably going to have to clear things up with the police, but we'll get home as soon as we can. It's Christmas Eve and we have so much to be thankful for." The woman stood and looked at the crowd that had gathered around. "Who do I thank for bringing my boy home?"

Jo stepped forward. "It was a team effort, but unfortunately, the man who started the ball rolling isn't here any longer."

Jerome pulled away from his mom's grip and walked to Jo. She squatted down and her heart dissolved when he wrapped his arms around her neck and whispered, "If he comes back, tell God I said thank you."

BOOKS BY DEBBIE

Warped Ambition

Warped Passage (set for release in 2019)

ABOUT DEBBIE

Debbie TenBrink grew up on a farm in West Michigan where her family has lived for 175 years. She still lives within five miles of her childhood home with her husband, kids, and faithful dog, Mojo. She has a Master's degree in career and technical education, and taught at two local colleges before settling into her career as a software specialist for a law firm in Grand Rapids.

Her first novel, *Warped Ambition*, was released in 2016 by Red Adept Publishing. The sequel, *Warped Passage*, will be released in early 2019. Her short story, *My Name is Diane*, was the People's Choice winner in the 2018 Write Michigan short story contest and is featured in the 2018 Write Michigan Anthology.

When she isn't writing, Debbie's favorite times are spent painting, camping, hiking, and watching her kids play sports. Regardless of what else she is doing, the lives and trials of the characters that live in her head are never far from her mind.

GET IN TOUCH

Website: http://debbietenbrink.wixsite.com/author
FaceBook: https://www.facebook.com/authordebbietenbrink/
Instagram: DebbieTenBrink (@authordebbietenbrink)

Literally Christmas

BY C. STREETLIGHTS

Natalie looked up and groaned at the shining faces of expectant children and their impatient parents. Tugging at her red-and-white-striped tights, she closed her eyes and tried to hide the annoyance on her face.

Mason, her shift partner, elbowed her in the ribs. "Elves are jolly, Natalie. You do *not* look jolly. You look constipated."

"I hate this job," she said through gritted teeth. "I look like an idiot!" She gestured at the green velvet dress that fell just above her knees.

Natalie would have looked idiotic if she were anywhere else. Her elfin shoes paired with the tights were ridiculous, and the bells on her wrists seemed cartoonish. Yet she looked stylish standing next to Santa Claus's red-and-gold chair at the mall.

"I'm right next to someone else who looks like an idiot "

"Excuse me?" Mason interrupted.

She put her gloved hand on his shoulder. "I mean, you look great. For an elf."

Mason was the perfect elf with his dark-brown hair and a light dusting of freckles over his nose and cheeks.

Children eagerly weaved through the mall's North Pole on their way to visit Santa's Enchanted Forest, their eyes sparkling at the intricate decorations.

Natalie tried to understand the reasoning behind the mall's commitment to the Forest. After all, more adults bringing their children to see Santa meant more money spent in the stores, but that wasn't always the case.

"What's the point of all this? Half these people don't even stick around to shop. They come in, get free pictures of their kids with Santa, and hurry out of the mall," Natalie complained.

Mason smiled and waved at the children. "Natalie, have you ever thought they do it because they want it to be a special time of year for the community?"

She rolled her eyes. "Oh yeah, and Santa can actually visit every home in one night."

"He really can!" a little boy said, clapping his hands.

Natalie bit her tongue. As much as she hated Christmas and all its happy trappings, cynicism was not to be shared with the public, including the children.

"You are absolutely right," she said with her best elfish smile.

Mason handed him a candy cane. "Don't forget to keep an eye out for Santa on Christmas Eve."

Natalie dragged Mason behind Santa's chair. "Why do you encourage these kids?"

"What do you mean 'encourage?'"

"You fill their heads with nonsense. It's cruel to support these lies."

Mason's eyes grew flinty and his jaw hardened. "The world already has enough 'truth,' Natalie. Children aren't allowed to be children. Adults complain when children's movies aren't entertaining enough for the parents. Saturday morning cartoons are gone. Kids barely get recess."

Natalie glanced around. There were children everywhere, and they seemed happy.

"What does it matter if children get one holiday to believe in magic? It's *one holiday*! Let them have it and get over yourself, Natalie." Mason walked away to prepare for Santa's return.

Natalie crossed her arms and took a deep breath. Christmas was in a week, and she would never be an elf again. This was literally the worst job she had ever taken.

Silver bells rang, intermingling with the excited murmurs from the children.

"Ho! Ho! Ho!" Santa called out. "Happy Christmas, everybody!"

"Welcome back, Santa," Mason said cheerfully.

"Thank you, Mason! We're missing an elf. Where's Natalie?"

Natalie slipped into place. "I'm here, Santa. Sorry, I was just a little behind, thinking …"

Santa peered at her over his spectacles. "I see. Anything you want to talk about?"

His twinkling, kind eyes made her feel like he already knew what was troubling her.

"No, thank you. Especially not when we have all these children to talk to!" Her false enthusiasm stuck in her throat, and she began to cough.

Mason patted her back. "Are you okay?"

Natalie cleared her throat. "It's just a tickle. I'll be fine."

Santa looked at her and wrinkled his brow, genuine concern reflecting in his blue eyes. She had no idea where management had found this guy, but he came each year and refused to be paid.

Natalie turned to Mason. "Do you recognize anyone?"

Mason nodded toward the front of the line. "We've got the Thompsons, Johnsons, and Reynolds over there. And it looks like the Millers brought the grandparents for their annual family picture."

Her eyes widened. "How do you remember all these people?"

"I've been working with Santa for a while. Since high school?" He left it as a question, which was puzzling.

Natalie laughed. "You both have memories like cameras, I swear."

Mason looked at her, brows raised and mouth agape.

"What?"

"You laughed. You look nice when you laugh."

"Someone has to be the heavy around here," she teased. "Who's going to be Santa's bouncer if everyone's nice all the time?"

The line grew longer by the hour, but Santa only became more cheerful with each visitor. Natalie was losing her resolve to have more holiday spirit. Her cheeks hurt from smiling, and her throat was sore from fake-laughing.

The holiday spirit can just take a seat, Natalie decided. Being a bitch was easier.

"Natalie?" Mason carefully asked.

"What do you want?" she snapped.

"Can you get Santa more cookies? Only bring ones that aren't broken and *don't* eat any of them." He closed his eyes and paused. "I mean, it's no big deal if you do, but I don't think you'd like them. Er … I'm sure you'd like them. They're delicious! It's better if you don't because … because we only have enough for Santa," he stammered.

"Don't worry, I won't eat the damn cookies."

Natalie stepped into the little cabin behind Santa's chair. Retrieving a plate, she grabbed the metal tin that was supposedly from Mrs. Claus. They received a new one filled with beautifully decorated sugar cookies each week. Icing delicately traced each one in lacy designs and edible glitter. She placed six of them on Santa's plate.

"Dammit!"

Natalie held half of a snowflake cookie while the other half rested on the plate. Broken cookies weren't allowed because they would ruin photographs. She quickly replaced it and was about to dump it into the trash when Mason's warning filled her mind: *Don't eat any of them!*

Stupid Mason. She wouldn't have thought about eating them if he'd kept his mouth shut, but now all she could think about was tasting it. Shoving it into her mouth, Natalie closed her eyes in appreciation. It was as delicious as it was beautiful. The buttery cookie melted in her mouth, the icing a perfect balance of sweetness.

Hurriedly wiping her hands and mouth, she looked in the mirror to see if she'd grown another head from eating the forbidden cookie and took the plate to Santa. He winked at her as if he knew, but she knew that was impossible.

Mason immediately approached her. "Did you eat a cookie?"

Natalie laughed. "No, I didn't eat a cookie! Why are you so protective of them?" She laughed again, but her laugh didn't sound the same. Putting her hand over mouth, she looked around to see if anyone had noticed.

"You ate a cookie. Dammit, Natalie, I tell you not to do one thing …" He took off his cap and ran his fingers through his hair. "Maybe it won't be so bad if it was just one," he mumbled.

"You're worrying for nothing, Mason."

For the rest of the day, Natalie noticed each child's smile and giggle. She witnessed every parent who became teary-eyed when Santa interacted with their child and remembered their names. For the first time, Natalie didn't feel annoyed or short-tempered.

When it was closing time, they said farewell to Santa and security walked the elves to their cars.

"Be careful with what you say, Natalie," Mason warned.

"Why?"

"Because you ate a cookie. I know you did."

"What's going to happen, Mason? Is a gang of elves going to come and bust my kneecaps?"

He sighed. "Just … be careful. I'll see you tomorrow."

Natalie laughed. "It's not like I'm going to go around demanding the twelve gifts of Christmas or something. Goodnight."

Mason groaned. "Oh God … no …"

Natalie stretched and enjoyed the warmth of her bed, the dream fading from memory. The dancing sugarplums that had occupied her sleeping thoughts waved goodbye and giggled as they disappeared. Never before had her dreams been so vivid.

Working for Santa must be invading my dream space.

Slowly opening her eyes, the scene before her came into focus. Six bundles of feathers were neatly piled on top of nests on her bed, their long, elegant necks twisted under their wings. Natalie gasped, waking the geese next to her. She crawled backward on her bed as one waddled up to her—revealing a nest full of eggs—and honked in her face, only to waddle back and plop down onto her eggs.

Natalie slid from her bed and opened her bedroom door.

Chaos filled her living room. Ladies were dancing between leaping men, drummers were drumming, pipers were piping, and girls were milking cows on her back patio.

She shut the door and tip-toed past the geese. Grabbing her cell phone, she went into her bathroom and found swans swimming in the bathtub.

"Mason! What the hell is going on?" she screeched when he answered. One of the swans honked in the background.

"You have swans, don't you?" he asked calmly.

"You know I have swans, dummy!"

"Have you found the French hens, the turtle dove, the—"

"*You* did this to punish me for the cookie, didn't you?" Natalie hollered.

"No, no, no! I told you to be careful, and you said something about the twelve gifts of Christmas! This is *your* fault!"

"You get over here right now and get rid of everything!" she demanded.

"I'll talk to Santa and see what I can do," he replied and hung up.

Fifteen minutes later, Mason walked into her bedroom.

"What the hell are you wearing?"

"What do you mean? I'm wearing my pajamas," Natalie said.

"You have elf pajamas now?"

"Oh my— What *am* I wearing?" Natalie looked down at her long, white nightgown with candy-striped ribbons woven into the lace. The tiny bells sewn onto the bows and embroidered candy canes were far too elfish to deny.

"Excuse me, Mistress," one of the leaping lords interrupted. "Your pear tree has arrived. I've put it on the patio."

"Oh, thank you," Natalie replied, then looked at Mason. "What am I saying?" she whispered.

Mason observed the chaos surrounding them. "Wow, okay, this is worse than I thought. You not only ate a cookie but you also have Elf magic in you."

"Shut it, Mason."

He held up his hands. "Hey, don't shoot the messenger. I'm just telling you what Santa said."

"You are literally telling me I'm an elf because I ate a cookie?" Natalie jabbed at his chest with each word. "That's insane."

"No, I'm saying you already *were* an elf and the cookie just made you more magical."

"That is the dumbest thing I've ever heard, and I don't appreciate—" She was interrupted by a crash in the living room. "Can we just take care of all of this," Natalie gestured wildly around her, "first? Then we can talk about that other stuff."

Mason looked at the mess. "Definitely. All you have to do is say what you want to literally happen. But not *too* literally. It's a balance. If you're too literal, something like this happens." He pointed to the swans.

Natalie raised a brow. "Wait, so you're telling me I got the twelve gifts of Christmas because I was too literal?"

"Well, yeah. You took the holidays and their meaning so literally that it was impossible for you to enjoy them. To you, if you thought Santa couldn't *literally* visit every home in one night, or if reindeers couldn't *literally* fly, there *literally* was no magic," Mason explained.

Understanding began to dawn on Natalie. "So I had to literally say something for it to literally come true for me to see the holidays aren't supposed to be like that?"

Mason smiled. "Exactly."

"Okay, what do I need to do?"

Mason took her hand and led her to the sleeping geese. Sitting next to her, he said, "I'm sure you know what to do."

"What? But I don't!"

He smiled at her. "You do."

Keeping her eyes closed, Natalie stretched and enjoyed the warmth of her bed. Mornings like these were her favorite, and luxuriating in the silence was something she treasured.

Wait.

Silence.

She hopped out of bed and ran to the living room where she found no dancing ladies or leaping men. There were no geese on her bed either. Her bathtub was empty.

Thank goodness.

Slipping back into bed, she thought back on the dream she'd had. It was vibrant and real, and it felt as if it had lasted hours. She drifted back to sleep for a while longer until she had no choice but to get up for work.

Natalie chatted with people in line for the Enchanted Forest and gave candy canes to the children. Her chest felt light, and she wasn't cranky. When she and Mason tied ribbons onto candy canes, she tied the bows quickly and artistically.

"You're in a good mood," Mason said as she made paper snowflakes.

"I know. I don't know why. Nothing has changed."

"You ate a cookie, that's what changed."

She rolled her eyes. "Stop. What is it going to do, make me an elf?"

He paled. "Why would you ask that? Of course it won't."

Natalie laughed but stopped when her dream came back to her. "I'm being careful with what I say, just like you told me."

"Good, I'm relieved."

"Yeah," she said slowly, "I'm trying not to be too literal." She raised an eyebrow, waiting for his reaction.

His eyes grew wide, and he grabbed her elbow and pulled her behind Santa's chair. "All right, what do you remember?"

"What do you mean?"

"What do you remember from this morning?"

"It *wasn't* a dream! I had swans and geese and milking maids … Oh my God …" Natalie panicked as everything clicked together.

"Calm down. It's okay." Mason hugged her, patting her back.

"It's *not* okay. I'm turning into an elf!" she sobbed.

"Who's turning into an elf?" Santa interrupted.

"Oh God!" Natalie wailed.

"I'll take it from here, Mason," Santa said. "Let's go for a stroll, Natalie."

They walked in silence for several minutes. Finally, when Natalie's hiccups faded, he asked, "Why do you dislike Christmas so much, Natalie?"

"I … I just don't see the point in the holiday. Everyone always acts so happy and cheerful, but that's not the way they are all the time. Why have a holiday for something we should be like every day?" She glanced at him and could see he was honestly listening, so she continued.

"I don't think it's right to let kids believe in something so magical and beautiful as Christmas when we know magic and beauty don't truly exist. Why do we do that to them? It's cruel," she whispered.

Santa looked concerned. "You don't think children should be permitted to have hopes, wishes, or dreams? Just *real* experiences?"

"How else are we to prepare them for real life?"

He was silent for several more minutes until they found themselves outside, standing on a patio.

"How old were you when you were adopted, Natalie?" Santa asked softly.

Natalie's jaw dropped. "How did you know?"

His eyes twinkled. "Let's just say I have a way of reading people."

"I was six years old and had been in the orphanage for three years when they told me I was finally going to have a real family. I was so excited!" Her eyes dimmed. "But having a family wasn't that great, to be honest. It was nothing like they'd told me it would be. It wasn't anything like what kids at school talked about either. We didn't celebrate any holiday because my parents said my sister and I weren't special enough. We didn't even have birthdays," Natalie explained.

"You just had a lot of real-life experiences," Santa said.

Natalie stood silently, his words hanging in the nighttime air. Were her life experiences the same experiences *all* children should have?

"Ready to go back?" Santa gestured toward the entrance.

"I think so, but I have a question."

He laughed. "Are you an elf?"

"Well, Mason said—"

"I don't think you're ready for the answer, Natalie. Mason is worried about your reaction if you know the whole story." He looked at her over his glasses. "What do you think?"

"I woke up with geese on my bed this morning, Santa. I might need time to process things."

He held his belly and tossed his head back. "Ho! Ho! Ho! I think you're right." Pulling a small snow globe from his pocket, he handed it to her. "When you're ready to know the answer to that question, the globe will tell you."

"But there's nothing in it, Santa. It's just an empty globe."

He winked at her. "That's what you think."

They walked back to the Enchanted Forest, and Santa nodded at Mason to assure him everything was all right.

Natalie smiled. "Mason, I'm fine."

"I just wanted to make sure."

"I feel great, and I'm being careful with what I say."

"That's super important. I can't be running around cleaning up after French hens."

Natalie laughed and knelt down to talk to a little girl standing in front of her. "What can I do for you, sweetie?"

"What do *you* want for Christmas, Miss Elf?"

"Oh, that is so sweet! Well, you know," Natalie looked at Mason and winked, "only a hippopotamus will do."

Mason groaned. "Oh God … no …"

BOOKS BY CEE

Tea and Madness

Black Sheep, Rising

ABOUT CEE

As a child, C. Streetlights listened to birds pecking at her rooftop, but instead of fearing them, she was convinced they would set her free and she'd someday see the stars.

Southern California sunshine never gave C. Streetlights the blond hair or blue eyes she needed to fit in with her high school's beach girls, her inability to smell like teen spirit kept her from the grunge movement, and she wasn't peppy enough to cheer. She ebbed and flowed with the tide, not a misfit but not exactly fitting in either.

Streetlights grew up, as people do, earned a few degrees and became a teacher. She spent her days discussing topics like essay writing, Romeo and Juliet, the difference between a paragraph and a sentence, and for God's sake, please stop eating the glue sticks.

Streetlights now lives in the mountains with her husband, two miracle children, and a dog who eats Kleenex. She retired from teaching so she can write, edit, and teach her children to pick up their underwear from the bathroom floor. She is happy to report that she can finally see the stars.

Her memoir, *Tea and Madness*, was first published in 2015. Her new memoir, *Black Sheep, Rising*, is now available and was selected as a 2017 Kindle Book Award Semi-finalist.

C. Streetlights is represented by Lisa Hagan Books and published by Shadow Teams NYC. For all press interviews and other inquiries, please contact Ms. Hagan directly.

GET IN TOUCH

http://cstreetlights.com/
https://www.facebook.com/CStreetlightsAuthor/
https://twitter.com/CStreetlights
https://www.instagram.com/cstreetlights/

Father Christmas

BY TIMOTHY WOODWARD

"**D**on't forget *you* have to call *me*. Do you have my dad's number?"

"Got it." Matt shoves his arm between the front seats of the car so I can see his cell phone. He's added a new number in his contacts: *Sean at his dads*.

"You know, Mom, if I had a cell phone, I—"

She cuts me off. "We've been over this."

"I'm *literally* the only person at school without a phone."

"Is this really the conversation you want to have before you leave me for two weeks?"

"Ten days. I'll be back on New Year's Eve. And I'm not just leaving you." I turn so I can reach Matt in the backseat. Our fingers intertwine for a moment. Mom keeps her eyes on the road, but the corner of her mouth goes up. She doesn't have to say anything for me to hear her thoughts.

Seeing the *Welcome to Manchester-Boston Regional Airport* sign makes me realize this is about to happen. I am leaving New Hampshire to spend Christmas with my father. I'm leaving my mom, my boyfriend, and the snow for the relative warmth of Georgia, the company of a soon-to-be stepmom, and a screaming infant. And of course, my dad. My dad who doesn't know I'm gay. My dad, who I am going to come out to for Christmas.

The last time I saw him, he made a surprise visit to see me over the summer. Though I wasn't thrilled to see him—I actually got a job scooping ice cream so I wouldn't have to visit him in Georgia—I did appreciate he made the effort. My dad hasn't always been an easy person for me to be around. He likes sports, fishing, country music—you know, straight guy stuff. (I know there are plenty of gay guys who like those things, I'm just saying my dad and I don't have a lot in common besides our genes.) Also, there's the thing where my dad assumes any girl within 10 feet of me is my girlfriend. Awkward.

It took me most of the summer to get the guts to tell him none of my *girl friends* was my *girlfriend*, and none of them ever would be. But just when I was finally ready to use the words, "Dad, I'm gay," he returned to Georgia for the birth of my new half-brother, six weeks early. My dad left to meet his new son before he had the chance to meet his old one.

But I'm going to fix that. I learned a lot last summer, especially that coming out is hard, but never quite as hard as you think it's going to be. And even though I'm still not quite sure how my dad is going to take it, I think he's ready to hear it. I know I'm ready to say it.

My mom pulls our Subaru up outside the terminal. All three of us hop out and begin the "airport waltz," rushing around the vehicle to grab bags and exchange hugs before an airport police officer can decide we've lingered long enough. By the back hatch, Matt is already pulling out my suitcase.

"Ten days? This thing feels heavy enough for a month!" He wrestles the bag to the slush-covered asphalt and extends the handle for me.

"Georgia in December is like wardrobe purgatory. Is it cold? Is it warm? Could be anything, so I brought my whole closet."

"As long as you don't stay in it while you're down there." Matt raises an eyebrow. He knows my plans and helped me rehearse what I'm going to say.

"You know me too well." I bite my lip. "I'm not going to chicken out. I'd be too mad at myself for leaving you if I don't go through with it."

"I know," Matt says. He leans over the suitcase handle and gives me a small kiss on the lips. Just a quick one. "For courage," he says.

My mom has been hanging back by the driver's door, but now she comes around to the back. "Don't miss your flight. Call as soon as you get there." She wraps me in her arms, her stiff winter coat crunching against my hoodie. "Merry Christmas. Take care of yourself."

244

The airport in Atlanta is huge, and it takes twenty minutes for me to find my way to baggage claim—but only twenty seconds to find my dad. He's tall, with a salt and pepper mustache and passing resemblance to Tom Selleck; he stands out in a crowd.

"Son!" Deep dimples form on both cheeks, and his mustache seems to double in size. He claps my back with one giant hand and pulls me into a half-hug. "How was your flight?"

"Not bad. I had a window seat."

"We're glad you came."

I hope he feels the same when I leave.

Twenty minutes later, we're on the interstate and based on Google Maps, we've got almost an hour before we get to the house. I had planned to use this time to get the deed out of the way. But now that my dad is two feet away, and I'm watching the rolling Georgia landscape fly by at seventy miles per hour, I'm not so sure. Do I really want to start things off like that? It's not like he can just turn around and put me on a plane back home. It could make for a very long ten days.

I must have been lost in my thoughts for a while because Dad says, "You're awfully quiet."

"Just tired." He seems to accept this, nods a little, and then reaches for the radio. Of course it's country: a youngish-sounding woman singing about a merry go 'round.

Dad breaks the silence. "Jill should have dinner ready when we get home. You hungry?"

I realize I'm actually starving. "A little."

"Your mother hasn't turned you into a vegetarian, has she?"

"No. I like meat." I turn my head toward the window to hide my smirk. That's not what I had in mind for a coming out.

"Good. Jill's got a pot roast in the oven. And true Southern cornbread."

"Sounds good." Out of nowhere, a surge of adrenaline pushes my heart into my throat. It's like my heart wants me to get it over with, but my brain won't let it happen. I open my mouth, not sure if words or vomit will come out. But it's neither. Instead, my dad is talking again.

"I know you'll like Jill. She's been looking forward to your visit." And just like that, the need to spill my guts has subsided.

"I'm looking forward to meeting her too."

A heady aroma of beef, carrots, and potatoes braised in red wine, rosemary, and garlic greets us as we walk through the side door into the kitchen of the red brick ranch. Jill greets us with a big hug.

"Sean! It's so good to finally meet you! I hope you're hungry." She turns back to the stove where she's putting the finishing touches on one beautiful piece of meat. I have to swallow to keep from drooling. "Leonard, show Sean to his room while I finish up here." Then to me, "Make sure you call your mother. If she's like me, she's waiting by the phone."

After dropping off my bags and letting my mother know I've arrived in one piece, I make my way to the dining room where Jill has done her best Martha Stewart. There are even cloth napkins in napkin rings! I didn't know people even used napkin rings anymore.

"Don't think we eat like this every day," Jill says. "This is a special occasion."

"It looks and smells amazing," I say. I sit down and grab a piece of cornbread from a towel-lined basket. "Where's the baby?"

"He's asleep," Jill says with a smile. He'll be asking for his dinner soon enough."

Dad chuckles. "Eat, sleep, and poop. That's a baby for you." He lifts a slice of roast onto his plate and passes the platter toward me.

The conversation drifts between college football (Dad's favorite team, Alabama, is going to another bowl game), fishing (tomorrow's dinner will be bass or catfish, depending on what we catch), and the baby (Jill hopes I'll be able to sleep through his crying). I don't really have much to contribute, and I keep my mouth full so I don't have to talk. It's not hard when everything tastes so good.

"There's chess pie for dessert," Jill says, noticing I take seconds of everything.

"Don't worry, I'll save room," I say. Chess pie is my dad's favorite, and mine too. We do have some things in common.

"So tell us about New Hampshire. How's school? Did you do the fall play?" My father takes a bite of roast and gives me a smile.

"It's good. We did *The Importance of Being Earnest*. I was Algernon."

"They're still doing that in schools?!" Jill asks. "We did that when I was your age! I was Lady Bracknell." Jill picks up her wine glass, sticks out her pinky like a "society lady," and adopts a high-pitched British accent. "To lose one parent, Mr. Worthing, may be regarded as a misfortune; to lose both looks like carelessness."

I pick up a piece of cornbread and join in. "Well, I can't eat muffins in an agitated manner. The butter would probably get on my cuffs. One should always eat muffins quite calmly. It is the only way to eat them." Jill and I laugh, and my father claps at our performance.

"I bet it was really good!" my father says. "I wish I could've been there."

"We sold out all three shows! And it was so much fun because my … friend Matt was Earnest." I got so carried away playing Algernon I nearly said "my boyfriend." That's not how I intended to come out. But then again, dinner is going much better than I expected. Turns out Jill is (or at least was) a theater person; surely that means she's okay with me being gay? Maybe now is a good time to do it after all. "You know, speaking of Matt, I should probably tell you—"

There's a sudden eruption of electronically amplified noise behind me, and I nearly jump out of my chair. Neither Dad nor Jill seems phased, and I realize it's the baby monitor sitting on the sideboard.

"Benjamin wants his dinner too." Jill stands from the table. "I'm sorry to cut this short, Sean." She hits the mute button on the baby monitor on the way out of the dining room.

As I help Dad clear the dishes, the phone rings.

Dad answers in characteristic Southern style, "Yello?" After a moment, he hands the phone to me.

It's Matt. "Hey, babe. How's your first night in Georgia?" His voice makes me smile, but with Dad a few feet away loading the dishwasher, I'm careful how I respond.

"Good so far. Turns out Jill is a regular Rachael Ray."

"Have you told them yet?"

"Not yet."

"Well, I wanted you to know I was thinking about you. Don't chicken out."

"Thanks." Our conversation goes on for a few minutes, but without privacy, it stays pretty G-rated. Even still, my face is tired from smiling so hard.

"Friend of yours?" Dad asks.

"Yeah. He's the one I did the play with. We hang out a lot."

"You gave him the number here?"

"I figured I might get bored." *And that I might need some extra encouragement. And I like to hear his voice. And I should probably stop procrastinating and just tell you I'm gay.* Of course, none of these things are close to coming out of my mouth. Instead, I say, "I'm actually really tired. I think I'm going to head to bed."

Dad nods his head slowly. "Good idea. We'll want to be up early for fishing."

It's still dark when Dad taps on the bedroom door, but I drag myself to the kitchen and the promise of coffee. Soon we're sitting side by side in his truck, a jon boat sticking out of the flatbed, heading to Dad's latest fishing hole. We don't say much, but my mind is reeling with ways to start the dreaded conversation. I don't want to bring it up too early or it's going to be a long morning. I don't want to wait too long, either, or I might miss my opportunity. And how does one start this conversation? It's really hard to just come out and say "I'm gay" without some sort of warmup. It's not like there's a book of coming out one-liners.

The sky is tinged pink when we reach the pond, and a layer of mist floats just above the surface. With the boat in the water, Dad gestures for me to sit in the front. Once I'm settled, he climbs in, simultaneously pushing us off from the shore. We head toward a half-rotten stump. The water is murky with sediment. I wonder how fish can even see in water like that.

"See if you can hit that crooked stick on the right there," Dad says, handing me a fishing rod. I unhook the *Tiny Torpedo* lure from the rod guide, set my thumb on the reel button, and flick the rod over my shoulder. The line zips out with a soft *zing* and the lure splashes just a foot from the stick. I still got it.

Fishing is the one activity that my dad and I share and I don't have to pretend to enjoy. He started taking me fishing when I was barely walking, and I'm pretty good at it. Plus, it's peaceful. Even when the fish aren't biting, it's like meditation.

I crank the reel, taking the slack out of the line. When it's nearly taut, I flick my wrist, and the lure jumps, making a liquid *pop* and a circle of gentle ripples. And then, the lure is swallowed in an eruption of water and scales; it happens so suddenly I nearly drop the rod overboard. But instead I jerk it up with both hands, setting the hook. The rod bends double and the fish starts pulling out line with a nylon squeak.

"Hooboy, that's a big one. Don't horse it!" Dad exclaims.

"I'm not!" Now the fish changes direction, and I crank the reel hard to keep the line taut. If it jumps while the line is slack, it could throw the lure. As if reading my mind, the fish explodes from the water, shaking its head like on the cover of a magazine.

"Don't horse it!" Dad grabs the net from the bottom of the boat. "Keep your rod up!"

I'm concentrating too hard to respond, reacting to each change in the fish's direction, anticipating when it will dive or jump, all the while reeling it closer and closer. When I coax it alongside the boat, Dad is ready with the net.

Dad pulls the bass from the net, grasping it hard by the bottom lip. He uses a pair of needle nose pliers to pull the lure from the fish's mouth.

"You had him hooked good." He looks at me with a broad smile. "That is one nice bass. Got to be seven pounds."

"I can't believe it. First cast." I'm out of breath with adrenaline and the effort of fighting the largemouth.

"I taught you well." Dad pulls a blue nylon stringer from the tackle box, and pierces the bass's lower lip. He ties the stringer off the boat, letting the fish back in the water. It fights for a moment, but the stringer holds. "Now that we've caught the baby, let's find the big one."

I chuckle at the joke; this is by far the biggest bass I've ever caught. Dad is practically glowing with pride, and I realize this is my moment.

"Dad? I need to tell you something."

"Shoot." He grabs his corncob pipe from his shirt pocket and smacks it against the heel of his hand to empty the bowl.

"Dad, I'm … I'm … I'm gay."

He doesn't react. Doesn't say anything. Doesn't move. But I know he heard me. The silence drags on for 5 … 10 … 15 seconds. Everything seems to have stopped. The pond surface is as smooth as ice.

Thump!

The fish on the stringer thrashes against the side of the boat, breaking the spell. Dad bangs the pipe on his hand again. He slaps it a dozen times; I don't think he'll stop until it breaks. But he does stop. He fills the bowl with fresh tobacco. Lights it. Puffs in silence.

"Dad?"

He responds by picking up his rod and casting toward the bank. The action turns him away from me. He doesn't need to say anything. I get the message loud and clear.

I barely cast my rod again. It feels like a lead pipe in my hands. Instead, I just sit, watching the sun rise above a stand of pecan trees on the east side of the pond. My father doesn't say a word the entire rest of the morning. Not in the boat. Not in the truck on the way back. When we get to the house, I jump out of the truck almost before it stops moving and escape to my room. I don't have anything to say either.

I refuse to come out, even when Jill knocks on the door and asks me to come to dinner.

"Your father told me what happened," she says. "You don't have to come out, but I thought you should know he cooked your fish."

I don't respond. I can sense she's lingering by the door. She says, "I made hush puppies and collards. I'll make a plate for you and put it in the fridge."

I'm hungry, but I don't eat out of stubbornness. Later, I hear the phone ring, and Jill knocks on the door again.

"Sean, it's for you. It's your friend, Matt."

I want to scream that he's not my friend; he's my boyfriend. I also want to run out and grab the phone. But leaving the room means confronting my father.

"Tell him I can't talk to him right now."

There's a long pause. "Ok."

By the next morning, I'm starving, and the smell of bacon very nearly coaxes me out. But my willpower is stronger than bacon, which surprises even me. Jill knocks on the door again to let me know she and my father will be out visiting friends for the afternoon. She invites me to Christmas Eve services.

"Thanks but no thanks," I say through the door. I don't need to be saved by their church.

Once I hear the kitchen door swing shut, I venture out to see if there's any bacon left. Jill has left a tray by the door, and when I lift the cover, there's not just bacon, but a waffle, some orange slices, and a small mound of congealed grits. I don't even care that the grits are basically wallpaper paste; I eat everything.

I watch some TV; *Rudolph the Red-Nosed Reindeer* is on. The stop-motion animation is hokey, but I used to watch this every year when I was little. It takes my mind off the disaster this visit has become. When I hear the truck pull into the driveway, I retreat to my room again, feeling not unlike Rudolph running away to the Island of Misfit Toys.

Christmas morning is gray with rain, which seems appropriate. I'm 1500 miles from my mother and my boyfriend in New Hampshire, where this depressing rain would be a beautiful blanket of snow. I think of Matt opening presents with his parents; both of them as supportive as possible. Meanwhile, I'm stuck with my father who hates me, and my well-meaning stepmother who seems nice but doesn't know me at all. I'm contemplating another day hiding in my room, when Jill knocks on the door again. This time she doesn't wait for a response. Instead, the door opens a crack, and then wide enough for her to enter. She sits on the end of the bed.

"Sean, I know your father didn't handle what you told him very well. But you should know he's trying."

"Then why isn't he here? Instead of you?"

"I don't think he's ready. I'm going to guess that you needed time to tell him, and just like you, he needs some time too." I don't respond right away. I realize she's right. I spent so much time thinking about me, what I was going to say, that I didn't stop to think about anyone else.

I finally muster a weak "Yeah."

"Listen, you don't have to, but I'd really like it if you'd come out and spend Christmas morning with us. I made cinnamon rolls." She pats my leg through the blankets.

After she leaves, I reflect that I haven't been fair to my father. Maybe I should give him a second chance. Even my mother needed a little time when I came out to her. Besides, there's cinnamon rolls.

My father and Jill are sitting on the couch drinking coffee. They've exchanged gifts and now have cinnamon rolls on small plates.

"Help yourself." Jill gestures to the plate on the coffee table. I grab a roll. It's still warm. "There's coffee in the kitchen. Can I get you some?"

I nod, my mouth full of my first bite. "Myesh blease." Jill gets up, leaving my father and me alone. For a second, no one says anything. Then my father leans over and grabs a small box from beneath the tree. He hands it to me.

"Merry Christmas, son."

I look at him in his flannel robe, salt and pepper hair still mussed. His disheveled appearance makes him somehow less threatening, more sincere. I take the box.

"Go on. Open it," he says.

It's just a few inches long and not quite as wide, but heavy for its size. I find the wrapping paper seam on the back and rip it open. I can't believe what I'm seeing. It's a cell phone.

"Do you like it?" my father asks.

"Yes. I've been asking Mom for one. This … this is awesome!"

My father nods. "I talked to your mom when we were planning your visit. It was her idea." Jill returns with the coffee and hands it to me. She gives me a wink.

"Thanks, Dad."

"I charged it up for you. You can try it out right now if you want." Something in his voice tells me I *should* try it out right now.

I pull the lid off the box. It's not the fanciest model, but that doesn't matter. It's my phone. I hit the power button along the top, and the screen comes to life.

Dad says, "I added in a few contacts to get you started."

I tap the contacts button, expecting to see his number and probably Mom's. And he has. But there's one more in the list. Right between Dad and Mom, there's an entry that says, "Matt."

I look up.

"Matt's your friend from the play, right?" Words aren't coming, so I nod. Dad says, "I thought you might like to call him first."

And even though he doesn't say it, the words hang in the air … *because he's your boyfriend.* My eyes feel warm, and I wipe away the tears with the palm of my hand. Dad gets up, gathering the plates and cups from the coffee table. He and Jill head to the kitchen.

Just before he leaves the room, he turns. "It's Christmas. You should always call the people you love on Christmas."

BOOKS BY TIMOTHY

If I Told You So

https://www.goodreads.com/book/show/13543211-if-i-told-you-so

ABOUT TIMOTHY

Timothy Woodward grew up in a small town in the White Mountains of New Hampshire and later moved to the city where he was a high school teacher and an advocate for LGBT youth with Greater Boston PFLAG. His students inspired him to write his first novel, *If I Told You So*, an ALA Rainbow List selection about coming out and finding first love.

Timothy has BAs in Cinema Production and Creative Writing from the University of Southern California and an MFA in Fiction and Nonfiction from Southern New Hampshire University. He currently lives in Las Vegas.

GET IN TOUCH

He can be found on the web at http://www.timothycwoodward.com/.
Facebook: https://www.facebook.com/timothycwoodward/
Twitter: https://twitter.com/timcwoodward

AND MERCY MILD

BY JUSTIN BOG

We all make mistakes. Around the holidays these mistakes beat with a pulse, amplified undercurrents. I try to make amends. My mother says this annoys her to no end.

In my teens, I never owned up to my faults, purposeful meanness, character flaws, or weaknesses—lack of a soul even. Yes, once I would've defined myself as a mean girl, a good soldier wielding barbs for a bee with higher status, ordered around by a cold and popular sociopath who didn't do me one favor. I wanted to fit in so much I became a shadow used for someone else's shade.

That's what others said about me, that I'm just as bad, and that I must've known. These gossips are strangers to me. I have a new last name through a second marriage to Ethan, and only those with killable curiosity search online to dig up my past.

My mistake?

Marrying trouble, a snake charmer of a man, the first to say he loved me, and he did, but obsessively (not in the stalker way, but the adoring way—I was his world), made me feel rebellious. I know he found this rebel side of my personality intoxicating.

We met at an Eminem concert when there still was a Palace of Auburn Hills arena. I was almost eighteen, yet seen as too immature by my mother to go chaperone-less to a concert that brought out a high proportion of the unseemly, again my mother's coloration of who attends these concerts. I'd been too dishonest during my high school years. My parents had every right to worry, but I was a fresh high school graduate, accepted at Michigan State University where I'd major in early education (and drop out before that graduation), with my whole damned life ahead of me.

At the concert, high up and far from the stage in the cheap seats, Jeremy and his brother stood behind my two girlfriends and I—these classmates were long gone and I don't go back to reunions. We were bullies, and even if we meaningfully apologized for misdeeds, we'd never be welcome at future gatherings. I glanced back at Jeremy too much. He wasn't watching Eminem, our hometown hero. All of us wanted to lose ourselves that summer. I gave this boy my number. He ended up moving to East Lansing to be closer to me. His brother roomed with him in a dingy apartment. They worked odd jobs and partied with fraternity boys, supplied drugs (they denied this to my face and Jeremy always soothed my worries), acted like they belonged there.

Jeremy and his brother, who instigated everything, every sibling plan, from mild to horrific, were altar boys from a Catholic church in Grand Rapids most of their youth, until they kicked them out for vandalism, graffiti—learning to attempt what wasn't right from a young age, to get away with it, that was the high they lived for—the brother (I can't even say his name anymore, can't stomach it) and I got along like feral cats, circling one another, never giving ground except to remain on edge. We agreed to avoid each other as much as possible.

Jeremy, after pursuing me for weeks, told me he had a sealed juvenile record. His tough-kid days firmly in the past, I didn't care about it because I believed him; he swore on his daddy's grave.

I married Jeremy. He said, "I do," with more fervor than I could muster; I felt at that moment as if I'd said my vows from the bottom of the deepest, waterless well. His brother was Jeremy's best man.

Even then, I didn't want my parents to be right, and that wasn't a sane reason to marry anyone. Only my dad attended if only to walk me down the aisle, and after handing me a slim envelope he wished me well and hoped things would get better. He didn't come to the reception. I emailed family updates to my parents, the rest of the family I no longer spoke with weren't sad at all.

The first time I introduced Jeremy to my parents, my mother, the rancid scent of too many whiskey sours wafting my way, whispered to me, "I don't see any tattoos." And then, later, "How can a nice girl like you fall backwards? We gave you everything."

"He doesn't have a single tattoo, mother." I sounded so weak defending Jeremy.

"Well, I see them all the same. He's that type. How serious is *this*? You've never introduced your boyfriends to us before."

"Too embarrassed to ever do that, mother," I said this meaning she would embarrass me, but she missed that, thought the reverse. My mother wanted to ruin this relationship, and I don't know why I didn't let her beyond me being a stupid punk, a young malcontented resting-bitch-face master. My only sibling, Chad (the second in a budding dynasty, making our father proud—he struggled up from dirt poor relations. Chad followed our father after learning how he'd invested all his superintendent money well in tech companies from the very beginning), remains estranged. Chad knew which side of his toast was buttered—he also didn't believe people were evil; he'd been shielded, protected— same family, different childhoods.

My parents talked to both of us when we were older. Told us how to behave if stopped on the street, in our cars, out in public. Be civil. Be courteous. Be kind. Stay alive. They'll twist your anger into something like a real weapon and it doesn't even matter if your parents have money. Chad graduated four years ahead of me, and then went to Business school at the University of Michigan. He now works for a boutique money management firm in Birmingham, the well-heeled city close to Detroit. He's married with two girls of his own. When we were on speaking terms, I could sense he and his dutiful wife, Savannah, would be terribly disappointed if their third child turned out to be another girl; he needed another Chad. I love my two girls. Toxic masculinity is a term I've embraced.

Back then, before the long Michigan winters grew too bothersome, my parents first retired to the posh side of Petoskey, where I'm sure one or two or more neighbors were unhappy solely about this, that retro-Archie Bunker mentality thriving in less diverse pockets of every state, one of the fanciest Lake Michigan summer resort towns (the show of wealth used to be anathema here), told me they didn't support my making the biggest mistake of my life: marrying Jeremy.

"Mom? Can Daddy Ethan take us to Disney on my birthday?" My youngest, Macy, asks this using a tone of sugary bewilderment, as if she's a Disney princess lost in a dark woods in search of a prince—she's almost eight and too old to beg for fairytale fulfillment. It's an affectation she's picked up from her older sister, Bonnie, who usually makes these needling requests. Bonnie's almost eleven, born between Christmas and New Year's Day, was old enough to remember that terrible Christmas in the past, where most of the time I couldn't stop crying.

"No," I say, with a warning attached. "Daddy Ethan and I make those big decisions together. Disney's too pricey to wait in the heat for hours to get an autograph from a pixie princess."

"I want to see the Lion King show!" More baleful whining commences. Macy's threatening tone works some of the time, testing my parenting skills.

Macy pouts for the rest of the day, sits in front of the television watching an animated sponge giggle and direct underwater traffic. The main advertiser on local cable during commercial breaks annoys, and Macy seldom mutes this one.

"Head on over to Rudy's Discount Christmas In July Extravaganza. We've gotcha covered!" Polar bears dressed like elves, animation far from the Disney standard, dance, as tiny penguins build toys (it's creative the first dozen times you see it). A Santa bellows orders with a twinkle. "Toys, toys, toys…games, games, games…dolls, dolls, dolls!" A screechy sing-song chant drills its way into my brain, "And for you moms and dads, we've got everything you'll ever need to trim your tree, brighten your home to a warm glow, make your neighbors envious by placing a shiny star on your chimney top (whoop whoop)! All at seven-tee percent off!" That's how the fake Santa says it, so obnoxious in this Florida haze. The girls find it hilarious how much the silliness bugs me and sometimes turn the volume to full Armageddon.

It's the beginning of July, just after the Fourth, one big bang of a day, and the Florida heat and humidity attack my soullessness—that's how I define myself these days, when I'm feeling sorry for myself. Macy'll keep making these suggestions until I wilt.

Ten minutes later, the commercial comes on again. I stand behind Macy in her favorite rocking chair. Her arms are so thin, wiry, peppered with energy. I watch while an idea forms, and then this new thought strikes me like a winning Lotto ticket.

Hurricane season'll begin within weeks and thank God we didn't lose much in the last one that passed nearby, a loose window screen went flying. Our own number will be called soon enough. I'm not a nihilist. I don't even think of myself as a realist anymore.

Later that night, when my second husband, Ethan, arrives home from his construction job, tired, his light fuzz beard speckled with dry wall dust, I tell him I want to make a change, a big one. Ethan's his own contractor, knows how to build anything, renovate old or historic, or damaged structures. He could be a one-man show, but he has a small work force grateful simply to have jobs.

Jeremy's mistake? Well, he had several, too many to list. His obsessive love forced him to make a stupid choice—forgive me repeating that—and his clingy obsequiousness became annoying. He and his brother didn't want to work, but took odd jobs around town, cleaning gutters, working the ski resort nights, grooming ski runs in northern Michigan, where we moved to be closer to my parents. Jeremy always said, "Family comes first." We could barely afford to keep the lights and heat on in a too-small trailer up near Cross Lake.

He wanted to wear down the wall my parents built between us. Over the years, two daughters joined Jeremy and I, along with increasingly petty arguments about how expensive babies, Jeremy said, "girls," were. I cleaned houses, and then took a job as a janitor for the Petoskey Middle School, the afternoon-to-ten shift. I think this embarrassed my mother the most, one of her gilded kids choosing to live in squalor (her descriptive). There were benefits, health care, vacation and sick days. The paycheck was meager for a family of four. Macy wasn't even one. Jeremy took care of the girls while I worked and then I'd relieve him. I'd sleep while he worked the night shift. But that was only during the ski season. Jeremy seldom found enough work in the summer.

Jeremy didn't do drugs. I told the judge that, and no one asked me if I did drugs. (Would I've lied under oath on that one?) Thank God. I wanted to be a character witness, tearful: "I know he did wrong, and he can never take it back. He's not a good person, but he's a good father to his girls. His brother probably made all these plans." I actually said that. "Objection, calls for speculation," was the response from the prosecuting attorney. I couldn't lie my sins away, rub out my mistakes from the ledger. I filed for divorce the day the judge sent Jeremy and his brother away for decades, may as well've been life sentences. By the time they're up for parole Jeremy's two daughters, Jeremy's brother's nieces, will be pushing fifty.

Christmas Eve happened, the day Jeremy made his most terrible choice, the worst mistake of his life, and he's paying for it. You can't kill someone, and paralyze a police officer, and think there won't be hell to pay.

On one of those prison phones with blurry thick plastic between us, Jeremy said, "I did it for us, for Bonnie and Macy, for you."

"I didn't want this. I need you to sign the divorce papers. Please, Jerry, the girls need this. I need this."

"I love you. You're breaking my heart."

"You broke mine a long time ago."

He actually cried. I'd seen this before. Big fake tears.

"What if I don't?" His smile sharpened.

"That's up to you, Jerry—"

"It's Jeremy to you now—"

I cut him off before he could say the nastiest things: "If you don't sign, you'll never see your daughters again. I'm thinking of moving south anyway."

"You bitch!"

He'd called me worse. I didn't visit Jerry again—that toxic man thing. He wasn't worth my time anymore. The girls ask about their daddy and I tell him he's on a long adventure, and that he misses and loves them, but where he's at he can't even write, can't even text. I changed all my numbers and I don't do social media. No cell service at all. He signed the divorce papers.

Jeremy and his brother, they both were bad seeds, but Jeremy's brother was the one who dealt drugs, made deliveries for a sketchy organization known to the police in northern Michigan, you name it he did it, had the Stooges-like idea to rob from the rich out on Harbor Point one Christmas Eve while everyone attended church services. They cased the place. Their bright idea? To give Macy and Bonnie gifts they'd jump for joy over.

The Point had a security guard, and things went wrong. Jeremy didn't shoot the guard dead. His brother did though, so Jeremy became an accessory to first-degree murder. Jeremy shot and paralyzed a police officer, and that's not worse than death, but comes mighty close, and all to steal a bunch of wrapped presents from an empty mansion on The Point to give to our girls. Macy didn't know what Christmas was yet. Bonnie expected Christmas and birthday presents, and her disappointment that year echoed from a cavern impenetrable by justifiable grief—loss of lives, loss of self worth, the splintering of families—because children shouldn't suffer the sins of their parents. They only wanted Christmas. My girls were on the nice list, and, still, bad things happened.

I met Ethan in a recovery group. I kicked an addiction to painkillers, something that wasn't a problem before that Christmas. I clung to the word spiral, as in, "She's spiraling out of control." My parents and sibling continued to fade into the past. My kids needed me. I didn't lose my job right away because the school didn't connect me to my husband—I kept a low profile, and I didn't clean with anyone else. I took the night janitor position when it opened up.

My only friend, who still spoke to me after the murder, lived next door. She was single without kids, young, and I could pay her ten dollars a night to babysit Bonnie and baby Macy. I came home and made her breakfast, don't know what I would've done without Sherry.

I took too many painkillers after spraining my right ankle sliding on ice outside our trailer. I went to a walk-in clinic. I stumbled in. My ankle wasn't broken, but it was severely damaged. They wrapped it after the x-ray, and the doctor who didn't offer a name or a look in the eye the whole encounter prescribed something that would relieve the pain, take the edge off.

Months later, I weaned myself off of these loathsome drugs with the help of a recovery group. Ethan was renovating the center's kitchen. I noticed how he watched others in the group, wore headphones. I wondered if that was part of his instructions from the group coordinators so he wouldn't overhear someone's sob story. He watched me, glanced my way. I looked down. I wasn't wearing my wedding ring. The divorce was ahead in my future at that time.

I bumped into Ethan at a hardware store, appropriate. I needed to make my own repairs on a door that wouldn't latch right now that Jeremy couldn't do these chores.

"Sorry to startle you," Ethan said, his face a blast of kindness. It's so natural for some people. A gift.

"Oh," I remember saying.

"Am I allowed to speak to you? Outside of—"

"I think so."

"I hope you're getting over whatever is ailing you. I've known so many people the center has helped. That's how I got the remodel job."

"It's who you know. Everything is." I sounded so down in that moment.

"Hey, do you have time for a cup of coffee? Don't want to trouble you, but I sure could use more caffeine."

I said yes, and Ethan became my confidant, the person who helped me place the past in perspective. I didn't introduce him to Bonnie and Macy for three months. I divorced Jeremy, and said yes when Ethan spoke one of his thoughts about the future out loud.

"What would you say if I asked you to make a new start? I hate the long northern Michigan winters, and my buddy says Florida needs construction crews especially now after the last tropical storm blew through. I've saved every penny and have enough to open my own company, wouldn't need more than one or two employees."

I didn't answer right away. I contemplated the move, a change of scenery.

Ethan told me he loved me. That he'd fallen for me, that he couldn't see spending the rest of his life without me. I heard my mother say, "You're a pretty girl. Don't let men take advantage of you." She always sounded jealous, bitter about it, made me doubt my own looks as she booked hair and spa appointments, did her best to fit in with those who did their best to conceal the fact that she would never fit into their structured lives—my mother wanted too much, fooled herself into thinking money bought acceptance.

I still didn't answer. I'd heard this all before.

"I don't want to just save you, Paige. I want you to acknowledge something, kick self-hatred and guilt to the curb, become the good person I've come to love."

"You think you're a hero."

"Well, I don't wear a cape for nothing."

"Up and moving. It's a big decision."

"Do you want an even bigger decision to make first?"

Ethan got down on one knee, took out a small ring box. As I opened it up, I broke down. I cried for the longest time.

I didn't think I was worthy of such kindness.

"Bonnie? Where's Macy?"

"Playing with Boo in the backyard."

"Will you ask her to come inside? Daddy Ethan and I have to speak to you."

"Another family meeting? Sheesh." Bonnie pushes buttons, playfully, testing invisible boundaries.

"Go get your sister, and Boo too." The neighbors in this starter-home planned community warn me about their deepest fears in the days after we moved to Tampa. Don't let your children or pets play outside unsupervised. Too many child predators on the street. Look them all up online. There are dozens and dozens, if not hundreds just being neighborly around here. Makes me ill to think about. And in the backyard? You always hear about some poor toddler taken away by the gators or squeezed by snakes, the real kind, the horrors of suburban Florida life. Why did we move here? Oh yeah, the sunshine and the fears of monsters from the swamp, animal and human. My parents retired to Winter Park, nearer to Disney, two years ago. My father emailed me this news. The lack of an income tax drew them south, not their grandchildren—but there has been kind of a sense of a thaw there. Chad stays in his chalet in busy Michigan.

Boo, our bull terrier, white with a black spot off-center on his triangular head, wags his tail and follows Macy into the dining room. He curls up on a dog bed in the corner as we sit at the table.

"Daddy Ethan and I have discussed something and want your help deciding."

"Sounds big, Mom." And then Bonnie motions with her hands, curving around an enlarged imagined belly.

"No!" I laugh, and in my ears my short burst of laughter sounds tinny from lack of use. "I'm not pregnant. Where do you get these ideas?"

"It's all over the television, Mom, the family shows. Whenever parents sit their children down for a serious talk it's either a new baby or a granny is about to move in, and since our grandparents don't like us—"

"They don't know you, and I'm working on that. They live pretty close now, and how do I know that? My dad, your grandfather, emailed me. Yep, he finally did."

"That is big news," Bonnie says with dripping sarcasm.

"Listen, girls, you aren't the reason your grandparents aren't speaking to me. It's their choice. They aren't bad people. We aren't bad people." I listen to myself as if I believe what I'm saying. "Hold up before I get too off course. Ethan? Help?"

"Your mom and I want to make a change, one that I'm fully on board with. Christmas is a time when your mom feels blue, like the old Elvis song you like." They know this. They know I'm silently crying behind my bedroom door on Christmas Eve. I fool myself by saying I'm not a prisoner to my past. I'm still giving in, being weak.

Macy and Bonnie stare at me.

"That's part of it. What if we changed Christmas?"

Macy and Bonnie's expressions of disbelief and fear appear.

"What?" Bonnie asks this.

"What if," Ethan continues, "we chose to celebrate Christmas in July, on the twenty-fifth?"

"Like the television says?" Macy's old enough to put two and two together, brainy, curious, and old enough to know Santa's a myth. We had that dashed-childhood-dreams talk two years ago after a snarky boy, a classmate, kept teasing Macy because she still believed in Santa.

"Yes. The Queen of England celebrates her birthday on a different date since it's so close to Christmas. I'm asking you to think about doing the opposite."

I take over. Macy and Bonnie are stone-face frowning. "Bonnie, your birthday is between Christmas and New Year's Day. What if we celebrated your birthday instead, for the whole week?"

"What about my birthday?" Macy says this, sibling rivalry a real thing.

"We'd celebrate your September birthday for a whole week too. We already have the best tree made by man. All we need to do is decorate the house."

"Even the outside?"

"Yes," I say, not really thinking this part through, but owning every change.

"Our neighbors will say we've gone nuts," Bonnie says, but she has the hint of a smile now.

"Can I dress Boo like an elf?"

"Yes," I say.

"Can we watch all the Christmas specials now?"

"Certainly," Ethan says. "The rest we can make up as we go along."

"Now, get your things. We're driving to that Christmas In July Extravaganza."

There's more to it than just this conversation. Of course I wrap simple presents for the girls come December 25th, decorate cookies, participate in their school pageants. But we don't concentrate on the holiday as much, and the pain lessens. The girls enjoy a big Christmas in July and a smaller one in December. Their schoolmates come over more in the summer, do holiday things, watch Grinch on repeat. We read "The Night Before Christmas" on July 24th.

Whispering later at night with Ethan, I feel hopeful. I admit that, and I ask Ethan about his parents, his siblings—maybe another mistake I worry over like beads is my hope to fix broken things. One sister still speaks to him, visits with her three kids for a Florida vacation away from that long Chicago winter they embrace. The brother-in-law is a peach of a guy. We have a lot of space for sleeping bags and a nice couch in our two-bedroom home on our stamp-sized lot with a view towards the highway and swamp beyond that. There's an ocean close by even if you can't see it.

"You've said it before. I once believed my parents would never bend."

"You read their email. Sounded like they may be willing to let down their guard."

"What about your parents?"

"They don't care enough."

"Because I'm who I am, the ex-wife of a murderer."

"Probably. They're too waspy to ever admit their own faults."

"Probably?"

"Well—"

"They don't like me, us, because I'm black, because you married a black person."

"I told you this long ago. It's nothing you need to keep talking about. It doesn't matter what my parents think. They don't know you."

"You know I think everything is my fault, that I need to apologize to everyone, even people I meet for the first time."

Ethan held me tighter. He's surprised me more than anyone I've ever met.

I remember not being able to breathe. That terrible night.

All the oxygen in the chilly trailer vanishing as if I'd been shot into space from home base, untethered—that's how I felt.

"Mom?" Tiny Bonnie teetered out of her bunk like Cindy Lou Who, not in appearance, but in how wide-eyed and innocent she sounded, simply kind and mystified.

"Sit down. Please, babe, I need you to focus," Jeremy said, scooping up Bonnie and placing her next to me on the cushion.

I took deep breaths, deeper down into that well that haunts me, the darkness, the depth welcome because it shielded me. My toddler-girl felt scared the next second as she witnessed her father fragmenting into manic desperation. Jeremy's eyes held a panic so severe it triggered my own.

After a moment, Bonnie and I clutched each other on the sofabed this late Christmas Eve. No, it was Christmas Day, the clock heralded a curse after its midnight chime. What was Bonnie doing up? That's where my thoughts spun to as my husband came home, stolen wrapped presents under his arms.

"Here. Take these and hide them." He said this and threw work clothes into a garbage bag along with his razor.

"What did you do?" I said, even as Bonnie grasped my leg tighter.

"Did Santa come?"

I ignored her question, pressed my hand against her bird-sized back.

"It's better you don't know. They'll think you were involved."

"Then take whatever's in those gifts back. I don't want to know, and you're not thinking whatever this is clearly enough. Take your troubles and leave us out of it. Is that your brother in the van outside? What did you two do?"

I heard sirens in the distance.

Afterwards, who could think about Christmas in the same way again? In the first month there were lots of cameras and reporters trying to get a shot of me, interview me, link me to what my husband and his brother did. They were murderers. I married badly. My mother was so right. She and the rest of the family shunned me completely after this Christmas, no more reaching out on my part either.

I stayed indoors as much as possible. I didn't park near work and somehow the newspaperman didn't stake out the school. I did tell my story to the principal. My side, and she had the best poker face, offered little reassurance that I'd be able to keep my job. If I became too big a distraction…

I'd sue if they fired me without cause. That's a thought I remember now. I didn't have the money to sue anyone, and no lawyer would defend me against the system.

I grew without solace, faced each day's questions with a stony demeanor. The girls became shadows joined with my own.

I visited the paralyzed police officer in the hospital, somehow avoiding the nurses and other staff members. Luck had nothing to do with it. I wasn't invisible, and I received side-eye from most of the all-white members of these northern towns regardless of how presentable I appeared.

I needed to move forward, and apologizing even if I didn't do anything wrong myself needed to happen. I felt this as the days passed. I read a story in the local paper about the officer's rehabilitation, the regurgitation of my husband's misdeeds. I needed to apologize for him. Maybe I am selfish. My parents think so.

I walked into the small private room, and there he was prostrate in bed. He was sweating. He didn't look diminished. That thought flittered in and then away like a hummingbird. It's the spirit that my husband had crushed just like his bullet had splintered the poor officer's spine.

"My name is Paige Pelecanos."

He struggled to move his upper body forward, placing his elbows beneath him and pushing. Anger filled his features. What was I thinking?

"I came to tell you how sorry I am for what my husband did. I wanted you to know that. Not a day goes by—"

The man screamed at me, all the vitriol of the world unloaded, and I took it. He shook his fist at me and became unbalanced on the hospital bed. I fled the room.

"You're a good person, a good woman," Ethan says, even now grasping, meaning well, but not fully understanding how I loathe compliments directed at me. He thinks he'll get through this barrier. Jeremy, behind his prison bars, probably wishes he'd never complimented me, never loved me as much as he did, never loved me at all.

"I didn't used to be." I had to say something. Sins can't be washed away, forgiven by anyone, not even a priest, not in my world. My own've left stains I've strived to bury.

"You're good now."

The glow of the twinkling holiday lights outside on the balcony brings little comfort.

"Our neighbors do think we're crazy," I say, and then, "Did you turn the Christmas tree lights off?"

BOOKS BY JUSTIN

NOVELS & NOVELLAS

Wake Me Up

The Conversationalist: Horrorstruck Novella One

The Threads: Horrorstruck Novella Two (coming soon)

COLLECTIONS

Sandcastle and Other Stories

Hark: A Christmas Collection

Speak the Word: Two More Sandcastle Tales

ABOUT JUSTIN

Justin Bog is a member of ITW: International Thriller Writers
Justin lives in the Pacific Northwest on Fidalgo Island, and is the author of psychological horror, mystery, and suspense tales.

His first crime novel, Wake Me Up, won a Foreword Silver INDIES Book Award and came in First Place for the Somerset Book Award!

Sandcastle and Other Stories, his first collection of dark fiction, was a Finalist for the Ohioana Book Awards 2014 and also named Best Suspense Anthology of 2013 by *Suspense Magazine*.

GET IN TOUCH

Twitter: @JustinBog
Facebook: https://www.facebook.com/JustinBogAuthor/
Website: http://justinbog.com

98128493R00159

Made in the USA
Middletown, DE
08 November 2018